Praise
Anthologies

'The longlist gave such diverse reading pleasures, yet every story, without exception, allowed me to enter worlds which felt carefully realised and full of possibility. As a short-story writer and reader, I don't need much convincing of the special power of the form, but these entries confirmed it once more – and most emphatically!'

Wendy Erskine

'An illuminating and vivid range of stories from an exciting array of new voices already so accomplished in their craft.'

Sharmaine Lovegrove

'I really appreciate the range and ambition on display in these stories. These are writers putting work into voice and craft rather than relying on event alone, and that's what makes their work persist in the mind.'

Chris Power

'One of the best multi-author short-story collections that I have read in recent years. An impressive feat, demonstrating the variety and power of the form.'

Jarred McGinnis

'A joy to discover these fresh voices in fiction. This collection of stories is exciting in range and originality, both in subject and form.'

Elise Dillsworth

'I was struck by the breadth, ambition and flair of the stories in the prize. This anthology presents a thrilling sample of distinctive new talent at work today and highlights some exciting emerging writers for us all to follow.'

Kishani Widyaratna

'Full of verve, emotional enquiry and imagination.'

Harriet Moore

'An amazingly diverse list. All the stories have their own unique energy, originality and power.'

Zoe Gilbert

'Eclectic, accomplished, bursting with life – an act of literature in discovery. It pushes and pulls the reader in all sorts of directions, yet remains centred around one consistent premise: the joy of the written word.'

Kit Caless

'Arrives and lands with thrilling confidence, quickly establishing an atmosphere that is subtle but indelible.'

Emma Paterson, on the 2019 winner

Brick Lane Bookshop

New Short Stories 2022

A BLB Press Publication

Designed, typeset and project-managed by Kate Ellis

First published by BLB Press in 2022
Copyright of the Individual Authors, 2022

ISBN 978-1-9162082-3-0

BLB Press Ltd
Brick Lane Bookshop
166 Brick Lane
London
E1 6RU

www.bricklanebookshop.org

A CIP record for this book is available from the British Library

Printed and bound in Great Britain by Clays Ltd, Elcograf S.p.A.

for everyone out there who reads
and loves short fiction

Contents

Foreword

Denise Jones

It can be risky starting a new venture, but in 2019 Brick Lane Bookshop took the plunge to set up and sponsor a new short-story competition, with cash prizes for the winners as well as a published collection of the twelve stories on the longlist.

I'm delighted that we receive hundreds of entries annually and have discovered some exciting new voices which are published in *Brick Lane Bookshop Short Story Prize Longlist 2019*, *2020* and *2021*. I'm also very happy that some of our short- and longlisted writers, including Huma Qureshi (one of this year's judges), have since been published by other independent and mainstream publishers.

Now in our fourth year, we have established a new company, BLB Press Ltd, to continue what has turned out to be a great success story. We're focused on delivering our original aim to find and promote new and diverse voices in short fiction and to work on a variety of ideas for publications in the future.

Kate Ellis and co-host Peter J. Coles have started to produce a series of BLB podcasts where writers read and discuss their work. It's fascinating to hear the ways people manage to find time to write in different circumstances and noticeable how committed they all are to their writing. We're also proud that music for the podcast is by Brick Lane bookseller Andrew Everitt.

Brick Lane Bookshop is working closely with BLB Press to promote fiction and short-story publications by independent presses. Due to the hard work and dedication of our booksellers, the shop is always busy, and we are delighted that more and more customers are keen to support independent bookshops where they can find books produced by small presses that are not always available in the larger chain bookshops. All of our stock, and access to the BLB Podcast, can be found on the website www.bricklanebookshop.org.

My thanks as always go to Kate, bookshop staff, all the readers of the submitted stories and especially the judges, who all spend so much time sifting and making decisions on the longlist, shortlist and the winners. Thanks also to the writers who submit stories. Long may the venture continue!

Denise Jones
Owner Brick Lane Bookshop Ltd
July 2022

Introduction

Kate Ellis

'I . . . had been paralyzed by the conviction that writing was an irrelevant act, that the world as I had understood it no longer existed. If I was to work again at all, it would be necessary for me to come to terms with disorder.' So wrote Joan Didion in her 1968 preface to *Slouching Towards Bethlehem*.

Perhaps it's the disorder of short stories that's often so appealing. They don't always make sense; they don't have to, they're only short. Traditional story arcs, characters, solid settings or plots are not always necessary or present. Yet sometimes stories require all of these, and also employ a traditional three act structure. They're unpredictable, they swerve about and wriggle like eels, slipping out of your grasp just as you think you've understood them.

Trying to figure out what makes a good short story is like trying to fathom what makes a good life. There are no rules, you don't know what'll happen, and you never know when external factors will surprise you. This, I believe, is what makes short fiction addictive and thrilling to read.

*

In this collection, we present twelve stories that rose to the top from 775 anonymised entries. It's difficult to sift so many high-quality submissions and we've had to let go of many wonderful stories along the way. By definition, reading and assessing fiction are subjective; there's zero chance everyone will agree to love the same thing.

Vivian Gornick says, in *The Situation and the Story*, 'Writing enters into us when it gives us information about ourselves we are in need of *at the time that we are reading* . . . As with love, politics, or friendship: readiness is all.'

I hope you're ready for the book in your hands. Each story it contains stood out from the crowd. It's a pretty wild ride and features a shaved horse, an Irish commune, runaways, a first sexual encounter, stranded sprats, a celebrity stalker, a European flirtation, a modern-day factory, extreme heat, a rugby-ball-shaped rock, Icelandic foxes, and a life in fast-forward.

The judges for the 2022 prize were extremely generous with their time and thoughts on these stories. It was a pleasure to work with all three of them: Anne Meadows was an editor at Granta for eleven years and is now an editorial director at Picador; Huma Qureshi was shortlisted in our 2020 competition, and her collection *Things We Do Not Tell the People We Love* and memoir, *How We Met*, were published in 2021; Chris Wellbelove is a literary agent at Aitken Alexander, where he was made a director in 2018. I hope that being read by these judges will help the twelve longlistees to prove to their families, friends, partners – or themselves – that they might actually be serious about this writing thing, and to find readers and even fans.

This year, we started the BLB Podcast to further celebrate and interrogate the short-story form. For each episode, we invite a writer to read from and discuss their work, how they write, and how they got published. So far we've hosted Isha Karki, Aoife Inman, Jarred McGinnis, Jem Calder, Wendy Erskine, Leon Craig, Niamh Mulvey, Huma Qureshi, Ben Pester, Vanessa Onwuemezi, Keith Ridgway and Irenosen Okojie. Each writer has different tactics for how to write: some do it early in the morning, some stack printouts under the bath, some do it while their kids are at nursery, some write in browser search bars, or on their commute. From every writer, we learn that writing takes a long time, there's no fast-track route, or magical secret, you just have to keep going and remain focused. The one thing that all writers have in common is that they take their own concerns and work seriously. They spend time editing and perfecting what they've written. They continue, over years. They try again.

Part of being a writer is contending with self-doubt, and writing anyway, because or despite of it. I'll quote Didion again because the greater the writer, the more comforting it is to hear about their wobbles: 'I sit in a room literally papered with false starts and cannot put one word after another'. But she found a way. I'm glad these twelve writers did, too, and I hope you enjoy these stories as much as I did.

Kate Ellis
Project Manager Brick Lane Bookshop Short Story Prize
August 2022

Brick Lane Bookshop

New Short Stories 2022

Missy Starling

Imogen Fox

If I were the kind of person who signed non-disclosure agreements and then broke them, I guess I'd start like this.

I had all but given up on finding the place. I'd been worrying that the snow and the barely sleeping and the stumbling out of motels into my car for yet another stretch of driving round Minnesota had been for nothing. Around midnight, some kind of highway hypnosis had taken over and I'd started to have visions of my frozen corpse being chiselled out of my car in the morning. But then I saw it. Or rather, I saw the walls. Normal people don't need walls that high – *especially* people in the middle of nowhere. Even so, I wasn't certain until my headlights floodlit the blue mailbox. The blue mailbox with a bird on top. Not just any bird: a starling. She'd posted a picture of it last spring. I was one of the five million people who'd 'liked' it.

It was the perfect spot. Off-grid. No reception for miles, and the snow, falling, settling, glittering like shattered glass, would keep most people off the roads. It had been hours since I'd seen another car.

I parked around the north side of the wall so my car

wouldn't be seen from the road. Had to give myself a little pep talk before venturing out into the snow. I'm a child of the South – Florida, to be exact. Didn't see snow in real life before I took my daughter up to visit the University of Pennsylvania. I said it was like cold sand and she laughed at me. Emily's at UPenn now. Full scholarship. That's the Ivy League one – some people get confused so I always like to clarify.

It had been days since I'd had real hope of finding the house, so I had to remind myself of the plan, and give myself a pat on the back for getting here. Self-esteem is really important and, when you don't have someone else to thank you, sometimes you've got to thank yourself. I'd arrived, I was at the house, and now it was just a matter of fiddling with the electricity box and scaling the wall. I'm making it sound simpler than it was; I guess I'm trying to sound impressive.

Now the crazy thing is that the back door was unlocked! What kind of person has a ten-foot wall surrounding their property, cameras and alarms and all sorts, but doesn't lock their back door? That's what happens when a celebrity wants to act like a normal person: they abandon their security team and they forget that normal people check their back doors. It's pretty adorable when you think about it.

It was maybe one in the morning and the house was – not dead quiet . . . sleep quiet. Like the walls themselves were breathing deeply. Trying to buy myself some time meant sacrifices; killing the electricity meant the house was slowly leeching its heat – you could practically feel the cold air sucking it out. I knew I had to move fast, but it's not like there was memorabilia or anything to distract me. I knew her Grammys weren't there – she keeps them in her house in Malibu. Same with platinum albums, old guitars, that dress she wore to the Oscars when she wrote that song for that superhero film: none of it was here. That's the point of this house: *Come November I'm heading north, back to where I can be myself,* that's the lyric. People don't pay enough attention to lyrics. If they did, there'd be a lot more people like me.

Still, memorabilia or not, I did find myself hesitating when my flashlight threw its glow over the furniture. Just thinking how this is her own personal taste, stuff she picked out herself. Being all off-the-beaten-track, she can't have wanted interior designers and stylists fussing around. No, that turquoise throw over the couch, she picked that. That purple baby grand piano – her choice. The stairs to the second floor had vines and flowers painted on them – and more were carved into the banisters. Shows you something, doesn't it – shows you she's someone who pays attention to detail. That was when I started to feel better. Especially because, those flowers, they looked like daisies.

Earlier, about halfway up the perimeter wall (second attempt – I got overexcited the first try), I had started to wonder if I was making a mistake. But as I searched for the master suite, nudging open doors to dark bathrooms, empty bedrooms, closets, I kept thinking about those little painted flowers. Deep down, I thought, hovering outside the entrance to the last door, she'd be glad I came.

That said, naturally no one reacts *well* when a woman they don't know wakes them up from a dead sleep. I

3

get that. I'm not about to get too upset about that. I'm a reasonable person.

Her eyes opened, squinty at first, then expanding like ripples. She didn't look so glamorous, pulled from sleep. Although her nightwear was pretty fancy for someone who was sleeping alone, I brushed it off as a celebrity thing. Still, for a second there she just kind of looked like your average twenty-six-year-old girl. That is, until I took in the torrent of blond curls, and those eyes – the kind of blue that shines. Even sleep-rumpled, she was still Missy Starling.

'Who the fuck are you?'

The language, I'll admit, I hadn't expected. She doesn't cuss in her music. I can't say I was super pleased – I do think it's the mark of a small mind to be using foul language – not that I'm precious about it or anything, I just expected that someone with the imagination and creativity to write something as beautiful as *Small-Town Hopes* would put her wide vocabulary to good use.

Anyway, I wasn't about to let her rudeness make me less polite. 'It's so nice to meet you, Missy. I'm Donna. I'm such a big fan.'

'Fuck. Oh my God. Fuck.'

'No, no, I don't want you to get upset. I'm not a crazy stalker or anything. It's not like I think we're secretly married – I heard about that guy who broke into your place in Malibu and slept in your bed. That was really terrible. I'm not about to do anything like that. I just want to ask you some questions.'

She made a grab for the landline by the bed. I wondered if she hadn't seen the hammer. It wasn't the biggest hammer, and the purple rubbering on the handle maybe made it look less intimidating. I'd bought it as a kind of gag gift when Emily went off to college; said I was going to knock down her bedroom wall, give myself one big bedroom. Maybe Missy thought she could dial faster than I could throw?

Just to be sure she had all the information she needed, as she raised the phone to her ear, I raised the hammer. She probably had just enough time to hear the lack of a dial tone before she saw the hammer, and dropped the phone. It tumbled off of the mattress and for a second there I almost knelt down to pick it up – can you imagine?

Once she realised that the line was dead, she calmed down a little. People are less stressed when they have fewer choices. If she'd been able to call the police, she would've felt obligated to, otherwise people would have blamed *her* if things went sideways and I turned out to be crazy. Now she knew that the power was out and the line was dead, I could see it was easier for her to slow down, think calmly. She sat up in bed, folded her hands in her lap like she was being interviewed by Barbara Walters. Her narrow shoulders shook.

'What is it that you want, um . . . ?'

'Donna, it's Donna.'

'OK, sure, Donna, why are you here?'

'You got a fireplace? This house is going to get real cold real soon, so I think we'd best light a fire if you've got one, and maybe you should put on some extra layers.'

You see? I'd come all that way, ready to get answers, but I wasn't about to leave her shivering while I got them. I waited, Patience on her proverbial monument (I bet you didn't think I could quote Shakespeare), while she slipped from the bed and rummaged in her dresser to find a sweater and thick socks and a bathrobe. She had some trouble with the sweater, her drawer packed so tight she had to tug it to get it out. Strangely enough, the drawer below that one was empty. I wanted to ask if it was some sort of feng shui thing, but didn't want to pry. Plus, I wasn't totally confident on the pronunciation.

She was smaller than I expected. All bundled up, she looked as young as Emily. There were holes in the wrists of her sweater that she jammed her thumbs through. Her nails were short, for guitar, not like those spiky long things some girls stick on their fingers.

Going downstairs was a tricky situation: do I let her go first or do I go first? If she went first, she might run off – not that she'd get far (I ran track in high school) but it'd be a hassle. If I went first, she could get hysterical and try and push me down the stairs. I would've understood that. It's not like we knew each other all that well yet.

In the end, I asked her to twizzle her bathrobe round, so that the knotted ties were at the back, and then I held onto them like she was a misbehaving toddler, while she went first down the stairs. She led me into the room with the purple baby grand. The fireplace looked more decorative than functional, but there was a pile of logs and newspaper next to it in a colourful wicker basket and she seemed confident enough when she started ripping up papers to build a fire. Made me a little uncomfortable, perched there on the couch while she worked, but I had to hold the flashlight steady and I didn't think we'd progressed to the point in our relationship where I could happily put down the hammer, so I didn't really have a choice.

'I knew you'd be here because of that song – *November*

Nights,' I said, feeling that the silence had gotten a little awkward. 'Well, and I follow MissingStars14, do you know them? They keep track of your private jet. I've been driving for days trying to find the place.' When it became clear she wasn't going to say anything, I explained, 'I don't want you thinking there's been someone saying something they shouldn't. You should be able to trust your people.'

She paused in her arranging of kindling, her hands shaking, but barely. 'I appreciate that, Donna.'

It was nice – the way she kept saying my name.

She lit the fire, and tucked herself right close to it; I suppose she was colder than she was letting on. I offered to pass her a throw pillow or a blanket to make herself more comfortable and she agreed. I had to let go of the flashlight, but that was all right, I kept it pressed along the line of my thigh, and besides, the fire was letting off enough light that we could see each other OK. She hugged the throw pillow to her chest.

It was pretty cosy actually. 'You don't get cosy like this down in Tallahassee,' I told her. 'That's not to say we don't have our comforts, but you don't get snuggled up the same. My daughter, Emily, she's up at UPenn – that's the Ivy League one, you know – she gets real winters.' I've wondered, more than once, if that's why she doesn't come home. If that's why she hasn't been home in three years: because it's hard to leave what you've never had before.

'It's the same in California,' she said. 'That's why I like it up here.'

There was a silence where I thought about Emily, and Missy tried out the shapes of words with her mouth. Finally, she said, in her soft midwestern voice, 'Would you like to tell me why you're here, Donna?'

Silly, isn't it? I was thinking about Emily, but I'd clean forgotten what I was going to ask her – or not what, but how. I'd practised on and off for over a week and now she was sat in front of me, looking like a lookalike of herself – not a pop star but the kind of girl who'd get stopped in the street and told, 'You know who you remind me of . . .' – well, I guess I'd got myself a bit starstruck. I think that's what made me a little clumsy in my delivery.

'You see, Missy, I wanted to ask you about Daisy Hays.'

Her forehead crumpled like a tin can; not what you'd call a camera-ready expression. 'Donna, I haven't spoken to Daisy in four years.'

'Far be it from me to call you a liar, Missy. But I hope you'll let me explain how I find that hard to believe. It's pretty obvious just looking at a photo of the two of you that you're more than friends. And then there's that video from the nightclub –'

'We were dancing!' She started twisting a long ringlet of blond around and around her finger.

'I've had a lot of friends in my life, Missy, and I never danced with any of them the way you danced with Daisy. Not to mention the kiss.'

Her hands went wide and expressive, the same way they did in interviews when she got excited. 'There was no kiss! It was a blurry photo taken from across a club. Not to mention, I have a boyfriend. Everyone knows I have a boyfriend.' Everyone did know about the boyfriend. Jake Swinton. People like me and Emily call him Joke Swinton.

'Uh-huh, and where's he?'

'Vancouver. Filming.'

'Convenient, isn't it? A boyfriend who's in the public eye but not in your home.'

'Donna, I'm sure you're a reasonable person. I know there are people who like to speculate about me and Daisy, but there's no actual evidence.'

She couldn't have set me up better if she'd been coached. 'But that's where you're wrong. You can't deny that there are any number of lyrics that are indisputably about Daisy.' This was the bit I'd practised. I was finding my rhythm, building my case. '"Kiss me in secret, love me in darkness" – why would a *boy* need to kiss you in secret?' I asked. 'How about, "Words flowing fast like a river through the forest"? Another name for a river: creek. Another name for a forest: wood. And Daisy Hays is the lead on what show? Oh yes, *Creekwood*.' I'm proud of that one. Not a lot of people online noticed that one, but I noticed. I went for one more. '"On a summer's day our love came into flower" – I don't need to explain that one, do I?' I felt like a lawyer doing closing arguments, waiting for a gavel to slam down and a judge to say, 'Well argued, counsellor.'

Missy didn't do that. Instead, she looked sort of sad. 'They're just songs.'

'But I'm right. I know I'm right. I brought a folder. I –' I realised where the folder was. 'OK, so I left the folder in my car. But there's just so much evidence – there are posts, there's, OK, so there's things like you'll post a photo with a candle, and then on that exact same day, a month later, she'll post a picture, *also* of a candle . . .' My words trailed off. It had all seemed so obvious, when Emily had

9

first explained it to me, when I'd collected materials for my folder, clicking through hyperlink after hyperlink on all those blogs, but saying it out loud . . . it suddenly seemed a little flimsy.

'Donna.' Missy's mouth twitched, a little peek of a too-white tooth, somehow reminiscent of a monkey baring its teeth at a predator.

'*Don't* laugh at me,' I warned her.

'I'm not!' she said, real quick, her face draining of colour. 'I was just – I wanted to smile at you, Donna. I wanted to show you that I get it. You know, I was like you. I used to be obsessed with celebrity couples. It totally makes sense.' She was nodding her head at me, and the movement was so jerky and odd-looking that, in that moment, I was kind of disgusted with her.

'You think you're like me?' I asked.

Nod, nod, nod.

Something she saw in my face, or maybe it was the twitch of my hammer, made her stop nodding. She crossed her arms, hugging them around her ribcage. She looked like middle-school Emily telling me she liked girls, like tenth-grade Emily coming home with a black eye, like a fuzzy college-freshman computer-screen Emily telling me she was spending the holidays with her girlfriend's family in Philly.

'You know we've met before?' I said. 'Do you remember that?'

She nodded again. I could have slapped her.

'It was with my daughter, Emily. The *Small-Town Hopes* tour. We were wearing matching T-shirts that said *Hope Springs*.' I'd screen-printed them myself with a kit

I'd gotten online. 'It was in Atlanta.'

'Oh yeah, I remember you guys. That was a good show.'

My teeth clicked together. The show had been in Miami. I guess in some ways there was a kind of triumph buried under all my wrath. I knew she was a liar; now she'd proved it.

I'd let our cable get shut off so we could afford the tickets. I'd done double shifts for three straight weeks so I could afford the gas for the drive there and back. After the show I was staring down the barrel of an eight-hour drive, but I stood in line with Emily, waited to meet her. I was in a strange frame of mind that night. Maybe because Emily was in her senior year and hadn't applied to a single in-state school. Maybe because she'd started skipping gym class because the girls wouldn't change with her in the room. So, when we were let into the little booth and Missy was right there in front of us, I vaulted right over my manners and went straight to, 'Sometimes my Emily thinks there's something wrong with her, you know, like she's broken or something. You don't think she's broken, do you, Missy?'

'*Mom!*' Emily had said, stretching the word into three syllables of horror.

Missy took it in her stride, and took Emily's hands and said, 'Of course you're not broken.' And that would have been enough. That would have been everything. But then she'd looked at me – no, not at me, *into* me – and said, 'None of you are broken.'

I wonder if the reason I'm feeling all out of sorts is because not once has Missy looked me in the eyes since I got here.

11

I realise I'm getting side-tracked. This isn't about me. It's about Emily. I'm doing this for Emily.

'Missy, I understand that you value your privacy.'

Missy snorted. She whipped her head round like she thought the noise must have come from somewhere else and then she clasped her hands over her mouth, like she could push the sound back in. 'I'm sorry. I'm sorry. I don't know where that came from. I just – I want to help you, Donna. But I can't give you the answers you want. Daisy and I were never together.' She knelt up a little, and I got the strangest feeling, like she was gearing up to walk me out. What did she think this was?

'You're lying!' I said. Except, well, it wasn't so much a statement as it was a little closer to a yell. And she flinched. And I felt all kinds of awkward. I tried to dial it back. 'Like I was saying, I understand you've got your image, and I get why you might contractually need to keep this kind of secret. But this is about something bigger than you and me and I'm not leaving here without proof.'

'Proof?'

I nodded.

'Donna . . . there is no proof. It didn't happen. I'm –'

'Don't tell me you're sorry! You don't know what I've been through. Look, my daughter, Emily, you met her, you know her. She's – she's dying, OK. She's got leukaemia and she's dying and she loves you and she's gay. She's gay and don't you see that you're – I mean I don't want to presume the specifics, but you're queer, you love Daisy, and if you could just give me something, I can let . . . let Emily go in peace.'

Missy looked so torn up that I almost took it back.

It wasn't totally a lie, though. If Emily *had* been dying, I would have done the same thing.

'I am so, so sorry about your daughter, Donna. And look . . . look, you tell her whatever you want, OK? But I'm sorry, there is no proof. Daisy and I, we were just friends.'

I couldn't believe it. For all she knew, my Emily was dying, and she wouldn't even tell the truth!

'No,' I said, standing up. 'No. That's not right. No. You wrote all those songs. You miss her. You wish you could be with her out in the open. *You put the colours of the pansexual flag on your album cover!*'

'Pansexual?' She crinkled her brow. 'Sorry, Donna, I'm not sure I know what that is.' Her voice was getting shaky, like in her concerts when she sings *Longing* and cries at the end. 'Donna, how about you put that hammer down and we'll talk some more?'

I didn't want to put the hammer down. I hadn't noticed I'd been swinging it a little, flexing my fist, but once I had, I realised how good it felt. Silly, isn't it? I'd spent so long in the car thinking about what I was going to say that I didn't even practise any hammer choreography. I tried some out now, smacking the head into my palm a couple of times. It stung. Missy flinching at the noise felt pretty good, though.

For a second her mouth opened, and then she looked at the hammer and closed it again. She seemed to shrivel, tugging on her hair and tucking her head to her knees. It sounded like she was muttering something to herself, and when I scooched a little closer I could hear, 'Fuck, fuck, fuck, fuck, fuck, fuck.' The more she said it, the more it started to sound like a sob.

'It's not going to be enough. It won't be enough,' I said,

trying to match the tone of a police officer interrogating a perp. 'Don't you get it? She's not going to talk to me unless I have proof.'

Missy just kept crying into her knees.

'Now, come on.' I tried again. The fierceness I had before was slipping away from me. Skittering out of my limbs and voice. I couldn't even threaten with the hammer because she wasn't looking at me. Her hands were balled up around her head and I wondered if maybe I should give one of them a whack – you know, just to show her I meant business. 'Missy,' I said, using the stern voice I used to use when Emily wouldn't put away her toys. 'I am trying to negotiate with you and you're not even trying to meet me halfway here.'

Finally, slowly, Missy unfurled herself and clambered to her feet, super slow like she didn't want to spook me. 'I'm – I'm really sorry, Donna. I'm sorry this is happening to you and to Emily, but there's nothing I can give you. I'm sure all she wants is her mom. You just have to be there for her.'

'How am I supposed to be there for her if she won't come home?'

'Look, if the doctors want her to stay in the hospital, I'm sure that's –'

'God, you're so stupid.' And then I really didn't feel bad for lying. *She* was the liar. She'd been lying to me, to Emily, to everyone, for years. 'She's not in the hospital. She's in Philadelphia. With *Amy*. Again. Even though she said she'd come home. She said.' My voice didn't sound like my voice. There was something hollow and screeching and broken that had clawed into my voice. I swallowed.

Tried to settle down. 'She won't even take my calls.'

Missy's mouth dropped open, and she didn't seem to know how to shut it again. She began the start of a couple of words, and then just sat down on the floor.

It was then that we heard it. The whistle of a door opening and shutting. A voice calling, 'Missy? You know your power's off?'

I knew that voice. I recognised that voice.

'Get down,' I hissed. Then I realised she was already down. I hustled on over to her, put one hand in her glossy hair and held the hammer over her head with the other. 'One false move and I crack you like an egg,' I told her. I was kind of pleased with the egg line. But then, listening to the sounds of footsteps getting closer, the occasional 'Missy?' called out, I started to wonder if it was actually a little funny-sounding. Maybe gave me away as an amateur.

Missy and I waited together. It felt like even our breaths were syncing up. I'd never been so close to her. Hadn't had my hands in someone else's hair since I last braided Emily's – so, three years. *Three years*. I sort of wanted to tell Missy, but then I remembered she was about to be in the mother of all time-outs.

The door swung open.

Here's where I want to get a little poetical. So, let's say the figure was silhouetted in the pale near-dawn light, a phone raised up like a beacon, the flashlight on, bright as a star, and in their right hand was a skillet. A cast-iron one – I'd eyed it up when I made my way through the kitchen, when I first arrived.

See, if you think about it, the clues had been there all along. The unlocked back door, the fancy pyjamas, the empty drawer. All the signs she was expecting someone.

Unfortunately, I'd been preoccupied, and hadn't put it together. And even if I had . . . well, I'd not been expecting *him*.

'You're Blake Bowdaniels,' I said.

'You're holding a hammer,' he said.

'You're *married*!' I said.

Well, we could've gone back and forth all day like that. Not that I'm what you'd call a Blake Bowdaniels fan, I've only seen a couple of his movies, but if I had to list facts at his face for ten or fifteen minutes I daresay I could do it. Except we got cut off. My phone started ringing.

'I thought there was no cell service,' I said.

'Not when it snows, but I can usually get a bar or two,' Missy said.

If I wanted to answer my cell, my choices were to let go of her hair or let go of the hammer, and I swear, I really would've rather held onto her hair. But I'm nothing if not practical, so I pressed the hammer head to her scalp for a second, released her hair, and fished my phone out of my back pocket. I answered without looking, not wanting to take my eyes off of Blake, just in case he tried any funny business. 'Y'ello?'

'Mom?'

She sounded crunchy as all get-out, but it was her. 'Em! You're calling me!'

'Mom, my card's just been declined . . . Why do you sound far away?'

'I don't have great reception where I am.'

'What?'

'I'm out of state, honey. And the reception's not too –'

'Mom, I'm getting like . . . every other word . . . I'm gonna call you back, OK?'

'No, Em, wait, let me –'

The call ended and I did an awkward little shuffle to get my phone back in my pocket. 'So . . .' I said. 'That was Emily.' I realised I still had the hammer hovering over Missy's head, and that felt more than a little silly now. I lowered the hammer to my side, and let Missy stand up.

'Donna . . .' she said, and for the first time she looked right into my eyes. I tried to duck my gaze a little, but she just kept homing in on me. 'There's a rest stop a few miles away. They've got great reception, and great burgers.'

'Good burgers,' Blake said. Missy didn't look away from me for a second, but she did something with her hands, and Blake said, '*Great* burgers.'

'Why don't you and me and Blake drive on down there?' Missy continued. 'You can give Emily a call back, and then we'll all head back here and you can sign some papers, OK?'

You see how this could be a great story, right? Inspirational, even. Like, no matter how messy the situation, there's always a way it can come out good. Maybe Emily was only calling because I had maxed out all her credit cards, so she'd have to call me for money. Maybe I smashed Missy's head in with the hammer. And Blake's too, just for good measure. I could tell you. Do you want that? Maybe you're like me and you want certainty. But there's knowing and there's knowing. Like knowing that the songbird and the actress are bound to get together – they're waiting out contracts or beating back managers, but one day, they'll be out and proud in front of all of us, and so long as you're waiting . . . there's always the chance of a happy ending.

Tipping

Giovanna Iozzi

In late July the heat dome you've been following on the news lumbers over from Canada, squats over London and refuses to move for days. Temperatures creep up past 37 degrees into the 40s. The humidity sweats your eyelids and you stop wearing bras. He has taken the kids camping on the Welsh coast, leaving you to finish a proposal for work and *to try to relax*, but the heat makes it impossible. You wander from room to room trying to find cool spaces in the house. In the last year, just like the Earth, your body has begun a slow-boil, to magic up tepid moisture on your chest, between your breasts, in the gossamer-soft creases of your groin, below the lip of your C-section scar. Recently, your flesh has developed weird hot spots as if someone is holding a match to some of its parts – calves, cheeks, lips, base of neck. Each of these spots seems to burn hotter when you are angry. Before they left, you had been arguing more than usual.

'You love conflict,' he said.

'Oh yeah,' you said. 'Can't get enough.' You licked your lips, made a canine sound. You both laughed, but it could have been crying.

'Are you OK?' he said.

'I may be losing it,' you said and when he tried to hug you, you pushed him away.

Perhaps you do feel more alive in the operatics of a row? When you surveyed yourself in the mirror afterwards, your cheeks were flushed with tiny broken capillaries in places, your eyes flashing, your lips murmuring excited curses. Your chest was moving fast, like you were drunk or turned on. The final issue was about sun hats. The kids – your boy, ten, your girl, eight – had lost theirs. How was it that all the ones you had bought had vanished? He had to buy some on the way, you growled, or they would all get heatstroke at the campsite. You think of their hair partings tenderising. As you do, you bite a nail down so much it bleeds a little. You bite down on other images before they start. Your children lying in a room with no food, no running water, dying of thirst. You wonder why you decided to have kids, a totally selfish act, if you think about it now.

Have you settled in? you text on the second morning.

Are they OK? Did you find hats? Sorry about all the shit.

He texts back, We have hats. Now relax!

Over the next few days, as it gets hotter, you start to shower three times a day, and take to wearing a white linen sack dress of your mum's, and although you feel sloppily middle-aged in it, it's the only thing your flesh can endure. At night you turn the pillow over again and again to experience moments of coolness; in the morning you sit on the edge of the bed and then get up slowly, your armpits already damp. The cats play dead in the front room, their jaws open, showing the jellied corrugation of their mouths. The male spreads his legs wide, his claws blanched chicken feet. You start to talk to them, and then in small moments to yourself. 'Hey fellas, hot isn't it?' They look out of their fur at you and say yes with their lemony eyes. You place bowls of water for them in different rooms which grow warm quickly, rejected.

They say brain fog is a real thing.

Brain fog is a real thing, they say.

It's a fog, they say, in your brain.

He says you repeat yourself more than you used to. One thing you read about was menopause and vaginal atrophy. A friend told you that once when she sat down, she felt herself split. But you are heating and flooding, all liquid; every few months blood drops out of you like your uterus is raining. Then the fire, which seems to shudder from your core and shatter inside the upper casement of your chest, driving its way up further into your head and popping into your cheeks as if a child has drawn bad red crayon all over your face. There are times when you are so hot, you imagine steam or even flames rising from the top of your skull as if you are a flambéed saint or she-devil, depending.

The leaves of the new fruit trees outside are bronzing when they should be gleaming green. One late afternoon you go out and fork up the earth around them, feeding water slowly from the can into the soil. The earth is like sawdust and some of the water pisses away its grey fingers into the gutter. You wear wellies and feel like a farm girl in the tropics. The

21

street is quiet, palpating in the heat. At first there appear to be no bird sounds at all, but then a scatter of lime parakeets screech over the trees. Kawa, kawa. They came in a few years ago – smaller bird species fled. In fact, you haven't seen a sparrow in a long time. Or a thrush. Or a robin. Or a blackbird. Ten years ago there were dozens. The pavement still radiates heat. You stand, your hand on the small of your back, looking up and down the street but there is no one about. You are waiting to see someone, a friend passing by, a neighbour, to be reassured of some normality. But it's still high noon, deserted spaghetti-western silence. It's 35 degrees and you know it will be another tough night.

Later, when the Earth balloons its fever, you touch yourself. You want release, the release you sometimes still get when time, the room, the bed seem to fold in on themselves like spatial origami. But now you can't seem to come at all, your body is hot and slippery and there's no traction. Perhaps the Earth will not allow you this release. She is heating, you are heating, there's no real break anymore. Maybe no one deserves to feel pleasure in the Anthropocene.

It's Earth-sized, the crisis. Too big. Your brain tries to wrestle with it. The planet is over 24,000 miles around. Almost 8 billion people. But you are not like Superman who flew around the world thousands of times, trailing strings of light, to reverse time. You are not a deity or goddess. Still, you imagine yourself as a giant woman, striding through the seas and cooling the globe by using your arms and skirts for shade, erecting high fences around the Amazon and the Congo Basin, throwing vast cooling nets over the oceans, pushing deep-sea trawler ships away with the force of your hands, snuffing out new gas and oil plants with your fingers. You feel angry that there isn't some magic you can do. You feel rage at the men who got the planet into this fucking mess and the fact that you probably won't be able to save your kids.

You are obsessed with weather forecasts, watching heat graphics lick over the UK on the weather app on your phone. Which is the most accurate? AccuWeather, XCWeather, the Met Office, the BBC? What's it like in Liverpool, Manchester, Glasgow, Skye? Milan, Paris? It's cooler in Spain than England, but the orange crops are decimated this year.

The weather men and women are smiling and joking as if this is a one-off event, promising it will break in a few days. They all seem to be getting it wrong while the heat doubles down. The women gleam and say phew a lot with mock gestures, stroking sweat from their foreheads.

They must know the science.

They've got to know.

Everyone in power knows.

By the end of the week, they say.

They say by the end of the week.

'This doesn't feel right,' you tell him on the phone. He doesn't respond. You have caught him at the end of the day with a warm beer in his hand. You can hear your kids' voices in the background, squealing about something they want, then their voices fade. They have made some friends, he tells you, they run in a ragged group around the field every evening. It's sweet and gives him a break, he talks to the other parents, he is getting lots of brownie points for doing it alone, he says, especially from the mums. He has to round the kids up each evening and almost strap them into the tent, sleeping bags half unzipped as even at night it's too warm.

'Is it bad there too then?' you ask.

'Not too bad,' he says. 'Bit overcast today, thundery, but still tons of people on the beaches. The BBQs fucking stink.'

This is geniality, this is getting on. You have shoved rolled-up facecloths under your breasts to absorb the sweat. Unusually you have tried on an old pair of vintage cowboy boots you wore in the 1990s, and as you lie on the bed speaking to him, you lift your right leg up and down, admiring the look of the toe and heel. You feel sexy. Maybe this is the moment to touch yourself again. His voice is low and you match it.

'I'm wearing the boots.'

'What?'

'Do you remember, my cowboys? The white ones.'

'Ah . . .'

He doesn't want to say no, he can't remember.

'Don't worry.' You have over ten pairs of boots at the last count, coated with dust in a cupboard.

'I've never known it like this,' you say, returning to your subject. 'I can't hear birdsong. There are no normal birds left.'

'They must be in the shade,' he says, his tone changing. 'Under the trees and bushes. Taking refuge – like us.'

He says the sea is like the Med, like a warm soup. Everyone's in the water. There were jellyfish yesterday, thousands of them, and people were screaming, falling over each other.

'It was like *Jaws* but in Porthmadog,' he says.

You laugh long and hard, a tincture too much.

The kids are tiring him out though. Your son likes to bury his little sister up to her neck in sand.

'Don't let her suffocate,' you say. 'Children can die in sand holes. The walls collapse.'

'Don't worry, I'm on it,' he says.

You think about the moment when everyone's back, all the needs crashing in at the same time, pots and pans, clanging in your eardrums.

My babies, I don't want them to die.

'I don't want the kids to die,' you say.

'What? Why would they die?'

'Starve.'

'We've got plenty of food.'

'Not now, but when –'

'Please,' he says. 'Not the bread-basket stuff . . . I can't . . .'

'Handle it?'

He can't handle it. Neither can you.

'You forgot her teddy. Is she OK without it?' Familiar ground.

He doesn't respond. See, the negativity put him off.

At the socials that are starting to happen, you experience the moment when people's eyes glaze over and they edge away. 'I've decided to stop flying, I feel so guilty,' you say. 'Don't you?' But you hear them speak later to someone else about their family trip to New York. They deserve it after the last three years, they want to see family and friends. Everyone needs fun and pleasure again. You feel like Fiver from *Watership Down*. Fiver with his nervous twitching, his wet eyes, his sweet neurotic mumblings. *But where is Hazel, listening, comforting?* In your head, Art Garfunkel's singing *Bright Eyes* and your eyes brim with tears. You wonder if people see you as Marvin, the depressed robot from *The Hitchhiker's Guide to the Galaxy*. Or Debbie Downer from *SNL*.

No you are Fiver, you are Fiver, definitely Fiver but without Hazel. You are trembling and wet all over. You wonder who your Hazel is – and you realise it is not your husband anymore.

It's a slow walk to the shops. The roads, the houses, seem to be holding their breath. You imagine paint melting, the grouting cracking and shifting. Heave, they call it. The air basks, bewildered. The plane trees, pollarded back like knuckles, have dry white dust on them, now useless and empty of birds.

In the supermarket the meat-locker light reveals humans in beachwear, topless men showing hairy nipples, wet curls of hair peeping out from armpits, women in complicated backless dresses showing small bulges of flesh under bras. Everyone seems to have earbuds in. No one is looking at you. But then, your face is red and for the first time in your life you're not wearing a bra in public and you have flannels tucked under your tits. The woman at the cash register flicks her eyes to your nipples and asks you if you want a free coffee.

'Is it iced?'

'No.'

'Then I'm OK thanks. This heat's intense, isn't it?'

'Yes,' she replies, her face stodgy under a severe fringe, 'lovely. Wish I was at the beach.'

'It's the climate crisis you know.'

The eyes glaze.

'I like hot summers.'

'Yes, but not like this.'

'Well,' she says, 'lucky you, to be able to enjoy it. I'm stuck in here – although at least there's air conditioning.'

'Yes.'

'Enjoy it while it lasts, love.'

How long will it last? Outside, you zombie-walk back into the blast of the street. Luckily your thighs are separated by some long granny pants. Your hair parting sizzles. You remember the documentary you watched about Karachi in Pakistan, where a young man fixed air con for the people who could afford it, and those who couldn't, including his own mother, lay in the heat of their small rooms panting. They were feeling ill and needed to lie down a lot. Some officials were painting the roofs of the houses white. There was a woman who was planting small oases of green where she could, but Karachi is burning up.

On your doorstep you find a dead swift. You crouch down, trying to detect a heartbeat in the fine geometry of its feathers, but there is nothing. You take it through to the garden and begin to dig a grave in one of the flowerbeds. Two summers ago, in the pale pink of dusk, you watched dozens of swifts wheel and flicker excitedly across the sky. They so delighted you, a man came to fix you a nesting box and you hoped, your whole body in a swell of hope, that some would start to nest high up on the wall.

It does not break,
    it does not break,
    and this is one week, just one week.
    When will it break? you ask.
    By the end of the week, the forecasters promise.
    But they are tired now, even the weather people. They've stopped smiling so much and are making smaller, floppier signs with their arms, as if the studio itself is warping. The weather forecaster has his shirt sleeves rolled up and tie loosened, his teeth are white and keep moving in a grimace, a terrible smile, like the Cheshire Cat.
    'Liars,' you shout at the screen and your own cats jolt.

At night the windows are open in all the houses on your street. You look out at the street lamp, trying to see insects. You recall a windscreen twenty years ago with insects piled up in crusted armies. You want to see swarms and swarms in the blue UV light but there are just one or two skidding around in the air. Opposite, in the first-floor flat, some people in their twenties are having a party. The music's loud. You are lying on your bed, the blind open at the bottom allowing you just enough of a view to watch as they drink late into the night. The women have long hair and bra tops. 'Fucking yes,' they shout when a tune comes on that they love. By the end they're swigging from the wine bottles and snorting lines off the table, a cheese plant casting tessellations of shadows on the walls. They kiss, thrash and embrace in the heat. You long to be in the room, to forget yourself for an hour or two. You remember clubs and dancing with him, grinding your hips together. He used to come up behind you and kiss your neck and jaw so much it would shiver your nipples into knots. At one point one of the men is hanging half his body out of the window, his torso sweat-bright, his voice seeming to join the clotted mess of the humid night.

Are all the other neighbours lying on their beds trying to sleep like you? The heat makes your body heavy, like a doll whose strings inside need rehooking. Your thigh sockets hang slightly, breasts loll like empty bagpipes. The temperature is somehow worse at night, as you expect release and it's like a planetary press bearing down on you. The orangey-brown dark is menacing, the Earth's core ordering up a nightmarish entrée from the future. Are the other humans naked like you, their body hair saturated, their limbs sweating in the stillness, like yours? Worries and anxieties looming like stone monoliths of the mind. The fan stirs the hot air around the room. Your eyeballs are hot. Your brain is cooking. Can a body start to cook? You will not be googling that.

On the fourth day, before they are due to return, you are hunched over your phone, scrolling through heat graphs and online data. Twitter is a screaming corridor of people who are very afraid. You read that there's more than 416 parts per million of carbon dioxide in the atmosphere, a fifty per cent increase since the 1700s. This is very bad. Someone posts an image of five giraffes lying dead in a circle in Kenya, their beautiful necks almost touching, like a withered jigsaw dropped a few feet from the sky.

Hell is almost complete, you think. Now what to do?

A daddy-long-legs skitters across the ceiling. When you were a child, on a caravan holiday in the 1980s, you got one caught in your hair. You cried out and made your brother smash it against the wobbly plastic wall. Now you watch this one, absorbing each jangly puppet dance of its body. It meets its shadow twin on the wall, jazz-shaking its long legs, then drops down into a corner of the skirting board and you try not to feel horror. 'Don't come near me,' you whisper, but then, 'Don't die, don't die.'

There was the summer of 1976. Naked in the garden with your mum, proudly pushing out your stout belly and chest. The heat was a miracle, an exotic one-off when London was hotter than Rome. Your mum and her friends wore their underwear as bikinis. You were all smiling, squinting into the camera. Mum brought out a basket full of beads and you wound them round and round your neck. 'It's like being somewhere else,' she said. There was your own birth, when you emerged from your mother's womb with teeth and your head full of black hair. You think of your own daughter, the way she burned you as she came out.

The next morning there is a shift, not sudden, just like an electric hot plate is slowly turning off. You remember the drama of downpours after heatwaves when you first met him, when the sky was refreshed and the earth smelt of petrichor. You remember making love with the windows open and rain lashing in. This is just a loosening of the belt, a slow outbreath; a sluggish rain dropping a scatter of wet. The walls at the front of the house are still baking when you put your hand to them.

*

He phones from a motorway service station to tell you they're an hour away.

'I thought you said it was unbearable?'

'It was,' you say.

'It feels OK now.'

'Yes, but it scared me.'

'The kids want to see you.'

You hear the agitated squawks of your children in the background. Your heart quickens.

You have not worked at all, but you will say that you have and that you managed to relax. You have bought a range of bamboo toothbrushes and a small pot of charcoal toothpaste. After holding the pot under your chin you dip the brush into the powder and feed its salty grit into your mouth. Halfway through, you see that your teeth are black, as if an ink cartridge has exploded in your mouth. You laugh into the pot which sends a fine layer of powder onto your white dress and the sink. You return the kids' plastic toothpaste tube back between the taps.

In the remaining moments of silence before they return, you allow one last fantasy to play out in your mind. Every microbead on sand, soil, sea and ocean, every rat king of plastic in every whale belly, every particulate in every city, every molecule in every placenta, begins unsticking, extricating itself, finding an exit, rising into the air, gradually levitating upwards through space into the blue ozone, joining a queue that begins its slumberous journey into another galaxy. Once there, it disappears into the mouth of a sluggish goliath who enjoys chowing down on plastic and farting it out into something alchemic. The world in an epic self-clean, a plastic resurrection.

You think about the plastic threading through the planet, you think about him and the kids coming through the door, their faces which now fill you with pain when you look at them. You feel sick for a moment, as though the room is tipping – the Earth, even. All the spots on your body flicker on. The pools on your flesh liquify. You feel your belly fire up and you lean over the sink as the flames begin burning upwards.

In Translation

Emily Gaywood-James

Your shared language is neither Spanish nor English. It is something unspoken, in which both of you are fluent.

'You must be warm,' she says one October morning in the playground, the first interaction you can remember. She nods at the denim jacket you're holding, while around you everyone is huddling inside their coats. 'I lived in London for a year when I was your age,' she goes on, her English perfect, though heavily accented. 'I was freezing the entire time.'

'It would be great to practise my English a little bit,' she says. The tops of her ears are turning red. 'I could help you with your Spanish, if you'd like?'

You go for tapas in the Albaicín. She knows a great spot, and you stand at a crowded bar, repeating words back to her as you explore how they feel on your tongue. You try *berenjenas*, fried aubergine drizzled in honey, two *tubos de cerveza* sweating on the bar next to you though you haven't learnt to like the taste of beer, not yet.

At school, you barely see her, spending most of your time with the teachers who need extra support in their

English classes. You repeat words back to the students so that they can echo your pronunciation, your accent sounding bizarre in small Spanish mouths. You play along when the teachers correct you, telling you you are mistaken about your mother tongue. In your training session back in London they warned you never to undermine *el profe*, so instead you smile and say, 'Maybe, but I've never heard it used that way.'

Each morning as you walk to school, your eyes snag on different details. In second-floor windows, *abuelas* are hanging out bed sheets to dry during the heat of the day, while on their doorsteps, grandsons smoke cigarettes, speaking noisily into mobile phones. On café terraces, the daily newspaper is left open at the sports page, an empty coffee cup sitting beside it, two stained sugar packets discarded in the saucer.

A couple of weeks go by before she asks if you'd like to go for *churros con chocolate* at Café Fútbol, and she laughs when you burn your tongue. 'I didn't know the chocolate was hot,' you say, your Spanish nervous, unsure. You lack confidence, you are realising, out in the real world. Half the time, even the words you do know stay unspoken.

She tells you she's going to stay with family for *la Fiesta de Todos los Santos*.

Your flatmates invite you out to a club that weekend, set high above the Albaicín with views over the Alhambra. It's a Halloween party, and girls get in for free. Men offer to buy you drinks and you laugh it off, unused to male attention. In London your undercut and tattoos make it obvious that your interests lie elsewhere. Here, though, men are drawn to your blue eyes and pale skin, approaching you with a casual '*Hola, guapa*,' and shrugging when you turn them down. You've heard comments about *las chicas inglesas* and you wonder whether here you've lost your identity, your nationality eclipsing your sexuality, an English girl but no longer a lesbian, back in the closet against your will.

The sun is peeking over the Sierra Nevada when you leave the club, the skies glowing pink, and you pass the city's early risers on your way to bed. Luckily, your heavy shutters block out all the light, and you sleep until 2 p.m. You dream of her.

It's still warm when she returns from her trip, despite it being November now, and she asks if you would like to join her class visit to the Alhambra, so you can see it the way it was supposed to be seen, rather than from a smoky terrace. You climb aboard a small bus and hold your breath as the driver navigates streets that seem impossibly narrow, far too narrow for the vehicle you're riding in, but he manages it and you're there, the city spilling out beneath you.

The tour is in Spanish, but the guide seems to be keeping things simple for the children, and you manage to follow the majority of what he's saying. Every now and then, she catches your eye from the other side of the group, and smiles, or widens her eyes, letting you in on a private joke you aren't quite sure you understand. At home, you slip your ticket stub inside the back of your notebook for safekeeping.

When you return from your Christmas break, she calls to invite you to the parade, though she doesn't mean Pride. '*La cabalgata*,' she tells you, 'to celebrate *los reyes magos*. The three kings.' The two of you stand in the Plaza del Carmen and you try not to flinch as the men aboard the floats throw hard sweets into the crowd for the children to gather up, their faces eager and excited.

You're already halfway through your year. Time moves differently in Spain, you're starting to realise. The bank opens and closes according to its own schedule, and you often find a paper sign tacked to the door telling you to come back tomorrow. Lunch lasts two hours, sometimes three, and she teaches you the word *sobremesa*, the time spent at a table after the meal has finished, talking and laughing and telling stories. You come to live by a different set of markers, quietly erasing the ones you used to know. The bleeping of your Oyster card is replaced by the tolling of the cathedral bells, ringing as you enter the school building as if to announce your arrival. When you get home, instead of listening to news of another teenage stabbing on the radio you listen for the arrival of the busker who plays beneath your window every afternoon, his fingertips strumming the first notes of *Here Comes the Sun*.

'It means pomegranate,' she tells you one day, and it takes you a moment to realise she's talking about the city's name. 'I never knew that,' you say, though from then on you start to see them everywhere: painted on street signs, carved into bollards, tiled into the pavements beneath your feet. You wonder how you hadn't noticed them before.

The next time you meet, she gives you a small book of poetry by Neruda that she found in a second-hand bookshop tucked away behind the cathedral. She says that studying poetry will be good for your language acquisition. You read it cover to cover, inhaling the musty scent of pages that have been turned by fingers before yours and underlining phrases that speak to you, trying to translate them. *Te amo*

*como se aman ciertas cosas oscuras, | secretamente, entre
la sombra y el alma.* I love you like one loves certain
obscure things, | secretly, in between the shadow and the
soul.

You tell her you've been translating the poems, though
you are too shy to tell her which.

'*Traducir,*' she says simply.

'What did I say?' you ask.

'*Trasladar. Trasladarse* means to move oneself.
Traducir means to translate.'

You nod, logging the correction. 'I suppose moving
and translating are kind of the same.'

She's watching you as you speak, saying nothing. You
are picking at the skin around your fingernail.

'I mean, the version of me that lives here is completely
different from the version of me that lived in London. I feel
like I'm in translation, in a way.'

She smiles. '*Eres una poeta,*' she says, her hand on
your forearm where it rests on the table. You know she's
teasing you but you are pleased all the same.

She asks whether you're staying in the city for *Semana
Santa*, and you nod. 'There's an incredible Easter procession
that goes through the city,' she says. 'You shouldn't miss it.'

You realise that the procession will be going down
your street, that you'll have a view from your tiny balcony.
Even before it starts, the streets are packed with bodies,
like Oxford Circus at rush hour. A few minutes later your
doorbell is ringing, and the two of you squeeze onto what
she calls your *balconcito* to watch the floats passing by,
your eyes drawn by all the colourful costumes. Her perfume
is sweet, floral. There's a crackle in the air between you,

and you try not to think about what might happen next, but when the procession has disappeared from view she tells you she's got an appointment that afternoon and has to go. You leave her wine glass on the side for the rest of the week, her lipstick smudged on the rim, not wanting to destroy the evidence that she was there with you.

May arrives, and she takes you to the Mirador de San Nicolás to watch the sunset. On the way back into town you wander through Sacromonte. It's 9.30, but it's still warm, your leather jacket rolled up in your tote bag. Whitewashed caves line the streets and, somewhere in the distance, you can hear flamenco music, sad and soulful. You want to follow the sound but she keeps walking and you're embarrassed to tell her you'd like to hear more. Soon, you're back on the cobbled street that runs alongside the Darro river, the lights of the Alhambra shining from above.

'I love the Paseo de los Tristes,' she says. 'I think it's the most beautiful street in the city. Showing you around these last few months has made me fall back in love with my home town. It's like I'm seeing the city through your eyes.'

You've been keeping a list of your favourite Spanish phrases, and over tapas at a small Brazilian bar, your confidence buoyed by a second glass of *tinto de verano*, you pull the crumpled piece of paper from your wallet and read them aloud. You wonder whether she realises these are all words she introduced to you. In return, she tells you her favourite words in English, and they surprise you. Homesick. Lovelorn. You ask her favourite words in Spanish. '*La madrugada*,' she tells you, and you smile, because you know this one. 'The early morning,' you say, confident at last.

To mark your last week in town, she invites you to a farewell dinner at her home. You've never been there before, and you carefully select an outfit, buying a bouquet of yellow tulips on your walk over to her neighbourhood. Your hand is trembling as you ring the bell.

A man opens the door. He smiles warmly, his eyes taking you in. 'Hello. I'm Paco.' He speaks slowly, carefully, and you can tell he's not used to speaking English.

'*Hola*,' you say, unsure whether to speak in his language or yours, but she appears in the hallway behind him. She kisses you on both cheeks and pulls back, her perfume lingering in the air around you. She seems nervous.

'I see you've met my husband?' she says, and he does a half salute.

Your eyes meet hers, and she looks down at her feet. Your shared language is neither Spanish nor English. It is something unspoken, in which both of you are fluent.

Whitebait

Martha Sprackland

People were down at the shoreline. Some with their hands
on their hips, or shading their eyes against the September
glare as they peered out at the water. Others were bent low
or crouching, tentative fingers extended to touch the wet
pebbles. Helena stopped running and took her earbuds
out, leaving them to dangle from the neck of her sports
vest. What were they all looking at? It wasn't usual beach
behaviour. She couldn't see anybody swimming, where
usually at this time (the tide was high and going out, the
distance over the pebbles from the promenade to the water
forgiving) she might've expected to see their blue or black
swim hats, or the inflated neon man-o'-wars they trailed
behind them as they swam – the serious ones, anyway – to
carry their phone, wallet, key. Though the air was warm,
the water was empty of people. But it wasn't that – the
strangeness was in the direction and intensity of attention,
only the backs of heads visible, every face turned away
from the land, the uncanniness of meeting no eye, catching
no expression. It was as if someone had pressed Pause
– though, no, they were moving, reaching and shifting,

turning slightly to each other, some pointing. But the quality of collective attention produced a sort of humming, as if a smudged reel of tape were catching on the spool. A gentle breeze cooled Helena's sweaty skin, and the small hairs on her forearms lifted. A lifeguard flag flexed briefly. She knew this unease, this spookiness. Twenty years ago, on a walking trip through France, he'd kicked her out of the van, and she'd hitchhiked along a lane that bordered a field crammed with tall sunflowers. Highest, blistering summer, July or August, her shadow short and shimmering at her feet, a stripe of sunburn on the back of her neck. And the crowd of faces turned from her, westwards to the sun, ignoring her slow trudge along the margin. Whether it was real or a later dream, a sunstroke nightmare sweated out on musty sheets in the tiny auberge in Angoulême, when she'd paused to drink water she'd seen one solitary flower swivel on its stalk to face her and fix her with its dark and compound eye.

Whether to stall that slowly turning gaze or from simple curiosity, whether to join that crowd or because she had run so far and so fast that her feet were throbbing, Helena came down off the promenade by the stone steps, and crunched over the pebbles towards the shoreline. The banks of chalk and flint cascaded underfoot, smaller stones getting into her trainers.

When she reached the water she saw what other people were seeing. Whitebait, in their thousands, were strewn across the darkened pebbles like scattered silver money. Some were still, their elegant little bodies draped limply over the stones like melted cutlery. But others, most of those Helena could see, were flashing frantically, dancing in an agony of airlessness, the effect of all those bright flickering bodies like code. It was spectacular, and it was unsettling. She squinted out at the waves, which were tall and glassy and green. Inside each as it drew itself upward she could see the shoal, or the idea of them fragmented, like the blurred impression through her front door's frosted glass of the postman delivering a letter. She went down onto her haunches and looked at the tiny creatures up close. They were flawless, tin-whistle clean, their gasping mouths worked in miniature. One by one, as she watched them, they would flop more slowly, then finally still and die. It took five minutes, six minutes, which seemed like an awfully long time. She could sense movement to her right; in the lee of the groyne a family group were playing rescue, scooping the fish in their cupped hands and flinging them back into the sea. The children scraped the bodies onto their plastic spades, breaking and bloodying them. She looked again at the frosted glass and saw this time the darker, larger shapes harrying the shoal, pushing it closer to the shallows, guiding the pliable ball of it as if shaping clay on the wheel. To her left a woman kicked off her flipflops and waded carefully into the water, standing still to watch the mob swirl around her shins.

Helena straightened and answered the phone that was ringing in her hand. Aixa asked her where she was, whether she was near the Co-op. Can you get peppercorns? she asked. The grinder's empty.

'Come down here,' Helena said. 'There's fish coming out of the sea.'

'There's what?'

'Fish. Little fish, all over the beach. People are throwing

them back in. I think it's stupid . . . they're dying anyway.'

'I can't come right now. I'm doing Cassie's bath. How weird, though.'

'Yeah. Sorry, I'm not near home yet. I had to come and look . . .'

'What are they?'

Aixa's voice came echoey down the line, rich with dove-grey tile and splashing water.

'Sprats.'

'Whats?'

'Whitebait. I think just babies. Herring, or something. I don't know what you call them in Spanish. I'll look it up. The mackerel are chasing them out of the sea.'

A green wave crashed noisily onto the pebbles and withdrew again with a hiss. She could hear the smack and giggle of Cassie splashing water over the side of the bath, heard Aixa's sigh and the squeak of her forearms over the tub.

'Hels, I've got to go.'

'What?'

'Are you home soon?'

'Yep, soon.' She crouched down again and touched one of the cold, silken bodies with her finger. 'I could bring some.'

'Urgh. No thanks.'

'I used to eat them when I was a kid, on holiday. Fried up, with a piece of lemon squeezed over.'

'Not for me. I don't trust anything comes out of that sea. Anyway, no fish.'

'Actually –' Helena began, but Aixa was talking.

'Hey –'

'– the water round here is pretty clean.'

'– hey. *Hey.* I've got to *go.* Get pepper, can you?'

'Pepper, yeah.'

'Leave the fish for the gulls. Cassie, stop it. *Cassie.*'

The call cut, leaving their daughter's name hanging in the space. Helena stood up and put the phone back into the side pocket of her leggings. Aixa was a bit squeamish. Helena glanced around, but no one was looking at her. The woman in the water stood knee-deep, her hands hooking the hems of her trousers up to mid-thigh, gazing out to sea as if watching for ships. The family to the right were packing up to leave, smacking grains of sand off the children's bare feet with a sock, as Helena's dad used to do to her and her sisters, after days at the beach, before putting their shoes back on. She watched for a moment, disconcerted by the memory. From the coast road she heard the dirge of an ice cream van.

'Fuck,' she muttered to herself, kicking a pebble away with the toe of her shoe. There was no reason for it to be this hard, was there? Her fault there was no pepper, her fault Cassie was being a monster, probably. Her fault they'd washed up here, on this sedate promontory of nowhere, this rocky strand, on the promise of work that it seemed clear now would not materialise. She didn't know how she had come to shoulder the responsibility for all of this, how Aixa could be both passively acquiescing and utterly fucking aggro at the same time. Hadn't they done what she wanted, only what she wanted, for five years? Hadn't Helena capitulated on everything, hadn't she said OK to vegetarianism, to dropping the old 'bad' friends, hadn't she said, finally, and without resentment, OK, *OK, then* to parenthood, to Cassie? OK, double back, then, to the Co-op. OK, no fish.

She stayed at the water's edge, the foamy waves stealing around her trainers and soaking through the fabric. Far in the distance the stand of turbines balanced on the horizon, gaunt and slow-moving. They looked larger from down here than they did from up in the town, some optical illusion, a trick of light or heat or air that brought them close.

A couple of fish flipped themselves over with a last desperate gesture. One, two, three, like leaves.

OK.

But she had nothing to put them in. Did she? She did. She unscrewed the orange plastic lid of her metal drinking canteen and poured the last of the musty water out onto the ground. Now she did not look around her, didn't care who was watching. Shuffling, bending down, then shuffling another step, she moved across the pebbles, picking up the tiny, cold bodies with her fingers and slithering them down into the dark interior of the water bottle. They tangled blankly in the bottom, eyes uncomprehending. They were hard to pick up, luxuriously slick, escaping her grip the way a dream, however vivid, might sift out on waking. Round, translucent sequins sloughed away and stuck to her wet fingertips.

The bottle carried a new weight. She stoppered it again and stood up, her thighs aching, and left the hundreds still scattered across the stones, the lowering sun lifting a last metallic flash from their bodies.

As she turned to make for the steps to the promenade she glanced at the few people still left on the beach. Not one now was facing her, not one looked towards the sea. She saw only the backs of heads, every face turned silently inland, some with a hand upraised to point towards the town.

'Great, Hel. Fucking weird honestly.'

Aixa was leaning against the counter, arms folded.

'Look, though.' Helena angled the bottle towards Aixa.

'I don't want to, thanks.'

'OK.'

'What are you doing?'

Helena straightened up from the cupboard, holding a sieve. 'I'm going to give them a rinse.'

Aixa stared.

'You're not going to eat them?'

'I don't see why not.'

In the silence there was a chirrup and rustle from the baby monitor on the countertop. Aixa spun it round and looked at it intently for a moment, then turned back to Helena.

'The sea is filthy. Pipes go into it, with shit. You know what I mean? Aguas residuales. Escorrentía.'

'Sewage. Come on, that's rubbish. There's no sewage outflow round here. You see fishermen all the time down there.'

'I see them, I see them, yes.' Aixa emphasised every word with a slow chopping motion of her hand. 'There is chemicals. In the sea. Helena, shit.'

'You don't eat them, then.'

'I am not going to, believe me.'

Helena shrugged and tipped the water bottle towards

47

the sieve. Nothing came out. She felt a sudden doubt – had she picked them up, really? Or only imagined it? And then she felt the weight of it shift, and the fish poured out from the dark mouth of the bottle in a cascade of silver that reminded her of the penny falls in the arcade. She remembered that he would press a five-pound note into her hand and go off to the bar, and she would go and feed the note into the change machine, press the button for ten pences so that what felt like a whole deluge of them would rain down into her hands. She would play until she ran out of money, or until he did.

She touched the whitebait with a fingertip. She heated oil in a deep-sided pan. Aixa went around the house opening all the windows, so that a breeze flowed into the house and over the bed like water as Helena got in next to the body that was turned away from her. She put out a quiet hand, feeling the cool of Aixa's unmoving back.

And, hours later, when she lurched from the bed to the bathroom and hunched over the toilet, cramping pain running through her body like fire, she heard the baby monitor screeching and Aixa shouting 'Te lo dije! Shit, te lo dije!' through the door, and felt the euphoric rush. How the coins used to tilt with promise behind the scratched glass, the wave of it receding and then coming on again and then suddenly the torrent, the cacophony of wealth, silver pieces falling and falling into her waiting hands.

Riding Lessons

Max Lury

Kieran met Nina on the steps. They were flat and grey and climbed up the shallow slope towards the house, which was all glass and clean white stone, unblemished. The sky was an open blue and the clouds were the colour of spit. Nina was smoking and wearing new glasses.

New glasses, Kieran said.

She nodded. Then, after a pause, she said it too. New glasses.

Kieran laughed. She had made the word 'new' long and hollow, like a tunnel, or a tube of dry pasta.

Then she stood up and hugged Kieran and said it's so nice that you've come, really. He said have you been in yet, and she shook her head. Gestured to the butt between her fingers. He nodded and took a seat next to her, folding his hands and squeezing them between his thighs.

Nina studied the end of her cigarette for a moment or two. She spoke without looking up.

Nervous?

You know, Kieran said, I haven't seen Tim in a long time.

Nina looked at him like she didn't buy it. Her black hair was cut short and it framed her face in a way that Kieran thought made her look like a celebrity. Not anyone in particular, just someone famous. Features you would remember.

She said is it the eating thing?

He paused, toyed with extending his silence. Decided against it.

Yeah, he said, it's still the eating thing.

She said is it still just in front of people, and he lied and said yeah, just people.

He had told her once when they were drunk and then in the morning he had texted her saying please don't tell anyone and she had responded of course not :) with a little smiley face that at first seemed mocking and then he realised, was a way of communicating something else. He didn't know why he'd told her. He could only guess. Sometimes he thought maybe he had told her because he wasn't attracted to her, because maybe there was nothing to lose by exposing that part of himself.

But he knew that wasn't entirely true. Once, he had convinced himself he loved her and he had drafted a whole message asking if they could meet up because he had something very important to tell her and then, in the same movement, his thumbs never stopping on the screen, he had deleted it all. When he woke up the next day he pushed it down inside himself until it sank, and the memory of the feeling now would come to him only for a moment, barely there, whilst he was on the bus or doing the washing-up.

There was space between the houses here, outside of London, enough room for bright-green hedgerows and flowerbeds. A squirrel stopped and stared at them, its head moving in little spasms. A yellow car drove past and Nina punched Kieran's thigh and said yellow car. Then they were silent again and watched the squirrel move in stops and starts across the lawn.

They heard a voice from behind them, and they both turned to see Ellie coming down the steps in an apron, waving a hand in an oven mitt and saying hello my lovelies. She had slicked her dark hair back so it was tight against her scalp and her free hand had a ring on each finger. Ellie gave Nina two big kisses and said her tits looked great and then when she gave Kieran a hug she did it slowly, like she was handling a porcelain doll. She squeezed his hand and looked him in the eye and said oh it's so lovely you've come, really.

Kieran put his hands in his pockets and said it's been a while and Ellie said yes, Tim's so excited to see you. Kieran was not sure Tim had ever been excited about anything. He thought it over as Nina and Ellie talked about something on the walk up to the house and then Ellie turned around and put her hand on Kieran's arm and said I'm excited to see you too, you know.

Nina said it'll be just like uni again and Ellie said oh God, I hope not. Kieran was not sure what Ellie meant and judging by the way Nina stopped for a moment he thought she wasn't either.

They hung their coats on a wooden rack by the front door, Kieran's a formless blue mass and Nina's sleek and black, almost liquid. As they moved towards the kitchen Kieran could smell something rich: meat, garlic, onions, pepper. Tim was stood behind the marble island with his hands in the sink and when he saw them he squinted like he was looking out to sea. He was shorter than Ellie by a head and when he stood next to her the effect was slightly comic. Tim placed the soap in a little china dish and wiped his hands, once, on a tiny cream towel.

Tim gave Nina a kiss on the cheek and then shook Kieran's hand. His were still damp and the hot water made them slightly too warm, like small sacks of blood.

Ellie said when was the last time you two saw each other and then Tim and Kieran looked at one another for a while. Something passed between them.

Kieran had not seen Tim for years, but they were still members of an old group chat that was pretty dead, apart from the occasional message. Kieran had never shared his shit on there but sometimes Tim would get very very drunk and say things like, I think about hurting myself more than you probably should, and someone would respond, yeah I think you're not meant to think about it at all, and then someone else would post a picture of a man with his cock out swimming in the Thames and say looks like he'll be telling the boys it was cold, at which point the whole whether or not you were meant to think about hurting yourself question would kind of fall by the wayside. Then Kieran would feel guilty and turn his phone on airplane mode and try not to think about it for the rest of the day.

Tim said I think it was at Katy's party I saw you last. Kieran had not been at Katy's party but he did not correct him. Tim said Kieran had been wearing a very extravagant hat and singing very questionable songs about dictators and their wives. Ellie made a dismissive motion with one hand and went to the sink to wash the vegetables. Tim looked at

Kieran and made a gesture like he was doffing an invisible cap.

Nina said you must let me help and Ellie said no, really, it's fine. Nina moved towards the stove anyway and picked up a knife and just sort of held it as if that was doing something. They were finding their feet, Kieran thought, trying to keep in time to a rhythm that had once been familiar but was now just out of reach, muffled behind a pane of thick glass.

Ellie said that she had just got back from Scotland and that she'd found the best veggie haggis recipe on Earth. She said it was a miracle.

Nina said nothing miraculous had come out of Scotland since Russell Crowe.

They stood for a while in the kitchen drinking wine. Both Kieran and Nina had brought a bottle, but Nina's was the one open, and Kieran's had been placed tactically all the way at the back of the fridge. Nina tapped her glass with a nail and said I really needed this.

Kieran watched them. He could see the people they had been ten years ago: the way Nina insisted on helping even though she had no clue what she was doing; how Ellie fussed over everyone's glass and seat until it was just right; and Tim, stood at the end of the island, watching, with a face that could not be read.

Tim and Ellie were an unlikely couple. Tim was kind of serious in a strange way and Ellie was, at university, very 'fun', which meant she did a lot of drugs. Sometimes she would just say things, seemingly out of nowhere, like, I'm that bitch. She would finish a glass of wine and hold it up to the light and say, I'm just that bitch. Tim could be awkward and was notorious for turning up to house parties and making small talk with girls about the technicalities of the stock market and then going on to outstay his welcome, sitting alone on a sofa long after everyone else had gone to bed.

But they made some sort of sense now, Kieran thought, they had an ease with each other which only came with time, and when Tim asked Nina if she was still on the fags Ellie wafted her hand in his direction like he was a bad smell and everyone laughed.

They sat on tall black stools which Tim said they never really used, and Kieran studied the lighting fixture above his head, which seemed to be a deconstructed stage light suspended on thick metal cables. There was a large stainless-steel fridge that imposed itself on the space and had only one magnet that said GRAND CANYON NATIONAL PARK in a font you might see in the Old West. The canyon itself was red and looked like a scab. At the bottom it said in white comic sans: JUMBO SIZE FRIDGE MAGNET.

Kieran thought that you were maybe meant to tear that off, but said nothing.

Nina was stood by Ellie who was chopping a romanesco cauliflower. She put her hand on Ellie's shoulder and they laughed about a friend of theirs who'd had a baby. Ellie wiped her hands on her apron and took out her phone and the two of them made cooing noises and stroked the screen with their nails.

The men were in their own pocket of the room. A space grew between the two of them and hung there, unfilled.

Tim nodded at the fridge and said she's a beauty.

Kieran took a sip of wine. It was heavy and coated his tongue. He gestured to the fridge with his free hand and said keeps it cold, I assume?

Tim laughed and raised an eyebrow.

It was always like this with Tim, Kieran was starting to remember. These half-jokes, stating the obvious in a way that made it ridiculous. Sometimes you'd talk to him for ten minutes before you realised the whole thing was a construction, that he was in some way playing a character who was meant to bore you.

Kieran asked what Tim was up to and he said ah, still with the asset management stuff, you know how it is. All very boring, really. But it pays the bills.

As he spoke the tips of his fingers traced the grey veins on the surface of the island, lovingly, as if the marble could respond to his touch.

Ellie clapped her hands and told everyone to take their seats. There was a small performance over who should sit where, and the couple argued for a moment about what they had agreed earlier. They took their places, the men at the ends of the table, the women sandwiched between. Ellie took off her apron and brought over slices of vegetarian haggis on a bed of spiced quinoa, with turnips and swedes that were a crisp brown at the edges, and apologised for the cauliflower being late. She said they could have it as a palate cleanser.

Nina said the food looked amazing but quite medieval, not that that was a bad thing. Tim said Steve Bannon says we're all serfs anyway and Ellie said right but I'm not exactly eating oats and grain, ignoring the fact that she was, actually, eating oats and grain.

Right, Kieran said, and what did Steve mean by that?

Tim winked and said Steve Bannon in a New York accent. Nina laughed and said Bannon again, but slower, making the 'a' sound into a high whine.

Then Nina said that she found Steve Bannon quite sexy and Ellie said that was probably actually quite immoral. There was a silence and Ellie filled their glasses again. Kieran watched the dark liquid fill his cup, and started the process of subtracting each drop from the next day. That was his routine: each sip, each mouthful, was taken from what he was going to eat tomorrow, bit by bit, until he had hollowed out each of the next twenty-four hours in his head.

Kieran felt like he should join in, make some sort of comment. But it was difficult to engage like this, two steps removed. He ventured that he could imagine Steve Bannon was pretty good in bed, and that he probably had a 'swinger'. Ellie rolled her eyes.

Tim stood up to get a beer and threw some of the plastic from the table in the bin and Ellie said recycling! in a loud voice. There was a pause and then Tim said he wasn't too bothered about the whole recycling thing and Ellie gave a big sigh and said can we just not tonight.

Kieran and Nina shared a look and then Ellie said well Tim did go veggie a while ago. She said it like it was something to be proud of.

Tim shrugged and just said I like animals. As if that somehow resolved the conversation.

Nina updated everyone on her charity and Ellie said that it was 'really impressive' and gave a thumbs up that was so bizarre it made Kieran wince. He had called Ellie stupid once to Tim, and said she just wanted to be seen to care, and every time he thought of that moment his insides seemed to shrink and pull away from his skin. He wondered if Tim had ever told her.

Someone had asked him a question and he only realised when Nina tapped the table by his hand with her nail.

Tim looked at Kieran and said, you used to talk a lot.

Kieran said sure. Probably, yeah.

Ellie said hey Tim be nice and Tim said I'm not *not* being nice, I'm just saying. He's got quieter.

Nina said I think everyone gets quieter with age and Tim said not me and Nina said we can see that, yeah.

At university, Kieran had been loud and Tim had been quiet and that was how they had been together. Tim had a genuine strangeness and when Kieran was either anxious or in large groups he could make Tim seem stranger, turning him into a caricature, and he could have the whole room laughing, not just because it was funny but because they all wanted to communicate somehow their discomfort at the way this small man talked and held himself.

And Kieran had savoured that feeling. Making everyone laugh, having everyone on his side for a moment. He thought all that time Tim had been laughing too.

They all ate a few more bites instead of speaking. Kieran cut up several pieces of the haggis but just moved them about the plate. Ellie stood up and said she had to check on the cauliflower.

Tim said can you pass the butter and Nina said what else's changed, Tim?

Tim said the butter, please, and then Ellie shouted from the kitchen oh fuck, fuck, Christ. The fucking romanesco is burnt to a cinder.

She came over holding the glass tray containing the bits of charred vegetable in pink oven mitts and said why do bad things happen to good people, as if they were all in agreement that they were, in fact, good people.

Tim said they could always order food online and Ellie gave him a look, like, don't you dare. Kieran mentioned you could pay for that with bitcoin now and Nina said she had no idea how any of that actually worked.

Kieran said don't you farm bitcoin and Tim laughed and said no no you mine it, and Nina made a joke about a poor Chinese farmer with a straw hat waking up at dawn to pluck strings of binary code from the trees and Ellie said that was maybe a little offensive and Kieran said ok but you do kind of farm it.

The conversation slowed for a while, swollen with wine, and pulled itself gradually across the next ten minutes. Kieran thought he could see the way it avoided him, parted around the topic of Kieran like a river around a stone. They had all pushed their chairs back so there was more space between them and Kieran watched the wax from the candles gather in pale orbs and then trickle down the long white stems.

Ellie said she was going upstairs to show Nina her paintings whilst the ice cream softened on the table.

Tim said he wanted to show Kieran something. His man cave.

Kieran laughed. I'm sorry?

My man cave, Tim said.

Nina said that's kind of sad, Tim.

Ellie laughed. She brushed Tim's shoulder with the tips of her fingers and left them there. It's our joke, she said.

Can you imagine Tim actually calling it a man cave?

Tim was beaming. That smile he always did when you couldn't tell if he was joking, if the Tim who had just said that was a character, some version of himself he was doing for his own amusement.

Ellie said she'd never been down there, that it was important they had their respective spaces. She had upstairs where she painted, her studio, with the north-facing windows and the hardwood floor, and Tim had downstairs. It's a trust thing, she said. It's like, I wouldn't want Tim watching me have a shit.

Tim raised his eyebrows. I've seen that a couple of times, he said. He rubbed his stomach and said Delhi belly.

Ellie said babe in a small, hard voice and then Tim was quiet.

The women went upstairs and then Tim and Kieran were alone. Kieran thought about saying excuse me, and leaving the table to make himself sick, but Tim stood up and cocked his head and Kieran followed. There was a sense of relief – the decision was made for him. The two of them made their way through the kitchen and Tim opened a white door that led down some battered stone steps into the cellar. They descended in silence, for so long that when Kieran turned back to look at the door he could not quite make it out in the darkness. He guessed they were maybe ten feet underground.

There was a small click and then Tim gave a push and a door opened. They stepped out.

The basement was all concrete. A single bulb hung from a thick black cable. It was cold and smelt of bleach, and, alone, tied to a square pillar that stood in the centre of the room, was a shaved horse.

As they approached Kieran could see that the horse's skin was the colour of the inside of a frankfurter sausage and when it heard footsteps it flattened its ears to its head and pulled away, as far as it could get. There was something dark on its ribs that might have been a shadow or might have been a bruise. The rope grew taut and strained.

What is that?

It's a shaved horse, Tim said.

Right, Kieran said, I can see that, yeah.

Kieran squinted. But what, he said, does it do?

Tim shrugged. Whatever horses do.

Whatever horses do?

Yeah.

Which is what?

You tell me.

Tim.

Kieran.

Are you deliberately avoiding my question?

What do you want me to say?

Ok, Kieran said. Ok.

Kieran ground his heel into the concrete and lifted his toes upwards. When he spoke again his voice was quiet. Considered.

But you shave it?

Every morning, crack of dawn. Tim said this with some pride, like it was an achievement.

Kieran stared at the horse, the vacant black globes of its eyes, the mottled curve of its hooves. It would occasionally shake its head and blow air through its nose. There was a white chalk circle drawn on the concrete around the horse, and, at the side furthest from Kieran, a faded brown stain.

What's the stain?

Ah, Tim said, *that*.

They stood for a while. Kieran chewed his lip.

So, Kieran said, what else do you do with it?

Ah, Tim said, you know.

No, I don't.

Well.

Tim inhaled as if he was about to speak but said nothing. They fell into an uncomfortable silence.

Tim walked forward and took a stick of chalk from his pocket, using it to smooth out the white circle around the horse, filling in the gaps, creating one unbroken line. He slipped the chalk back into his trousers and wiped the dust on his thighs. Each time he approached the circle the horse would pull back with a swing of its long head and turn its body away from him. Then it would move so that one big eye was visible. Watching them.

The horse gazed back out at the two men, all smooth flesh and small eyes, their tight faces, and the way the shorter one moved made it shake. It could smell their sweat and the sharp thin scent of aerosol and the wine that made their breath heavy. It gave a little stamp. Flared its nostrils. Memories surfaced as a tremor in its flank. It only knew the dark and the room and the man. It urinated a little.

Kieran looked at Tim, the funny way he had cocked his head, the way he had his hands now clasped behind his back as if he was in a museum or an art gallery. He wasn't smiling – but he wasn't not smiling; he was holding his face in a strange sort of stasis, a halfway point between the two that was neither and both. There was no way of telling.

Does Ellie know? Kieran asked.

Tim turned to him and tapped his nose, before clapping twice. Well, he said, that's enough of that. He led Kieran from the room, fiddling with a set of keys in a way that made them faintly echo from the cellar walls. Before Kieran left he turned his head to look at the horse, smaller now, its two eyes fixed on the exit.

The men climbed the steps and just before they reached the top Tim turned around and said it was very important to me that you saw that. Then he pushed open the door and the sound of music and the smell of burnt romanesco and gravy filled the air and there was no question of talking about it further, because Tim had put his arms around Ellie and was kissing her face and saying did you show Nina your amazing paintings baby.

Nina said they were honestly just magic, pure magic, and blew a kiss at Ellie and did a little wiggle of her shoulders, leaning back so she could see Kieran and patting the seat next to her with a flat palm.

Kieran took the seat. For a while it was as if the floor was made of glass and he could almost see the horse, alone now in the dark, beneath their feet, but as the conversation grew between them and Nina poured him another glass of wine, the image clouded over. He watched Ellie's face for a glimmer of recognition. A look she might throw him that would mean I know and there is nothing that can be done. But there was none. She was drunk and her eyes were just starting to get that absent gloss and her teeth were stained a dark red.

Ellie filled Tim in on the joke they had been having upstairs, something about Jodorowsky directing *Toy Story*, and as Tim joined in, doing the voice of the caterpillar from *A Bug's Life*, Ellie made her way into the kitchen and returned with dessert. She served prim scoops of coffee ice cream topped with chopped nuts on little rectangular slates and said it was a bit naughty but why the hell not. Kieran looked at his and hoped that if he just watched it for long enough it would melt and it might look like he'd had a few bites. He moved some around with the curved side of his spoon and pinched his thigh under the table.

Ellie looked up and said but you are ok, aren't you, Kieran?

She said it as if they had all been talking about this prior, like this was the natural conclusion to a conversation that until now had gone unspoken. The room went quiet and Kieran could feel all the objects around him as things that were very hard and very real, and the way they occupied space made him feel like he had somehow shrunk into the hollow behind his eyes.

It had been his decision to come, really. Nina had said they should do something now he was out – and he had noticed the way she didn't say hospital, as if doing so would fill her mouth with the taste of bleach and antiseptic – and she had mentioned that she still did dinner with Tim and Ellie sometimes and Kieran had no choice but to say of course that'll be fine, and when she asked again he insisted that it was fine, really, and then there was nothing either of them could do. She couldn't push it further without forcing his hand, and he'd been so keen to seem normal he'd trapped himself.

You know, Ellie said, taking Tim's hand, we were all very worried about you. Kieran thought maybe Ellie was trying to embarrass him. Or trying to help. Or both, he supposed, at the same time.

Kieran could feel Nina look at him from the corner of her eye. He could also feel that he was actually quite drunk. Tim didn't smile at Kieran but looked instead at his plate and said nothing. Kieran wondered what they knew. He pressed his hands between his thighs.

Ellie gave Tim's hand a squeeze and Kieran could see the faint trace of chalk on Tim's fingertips, catching the light, leaving tiny white flecks on the dark wood of the table.

Kieran had only seen Tim break his act once. But they had not talked about it on the walk back from the hospital in the morning rain, stopping every five minutes so Tim could retch and spit on the side of the road, and they had not mentioned it when Ellie asked with a kind of limp curiosity where they had both been the night before, and Kieran was definitely not going to talk about it here, now it had calcified inside him, and become something he only returned to in the dark.

He had not said anything for a long while. The ice cream had started to melt and ran in a slow brown stream off the slate and onto the surface beneath.

Yeah, Kieran said. I was just very sick for a while.

A pause. Nina finished her wine and pretended to have another sip. Tim looked Kieran in the eye.

Kieran did not want to continue. He wanted to keep all that to himself, and the idea of it, under these lights, splayed on the table like a dissected frog, all tendons and dark dense organs, made his mouth dry. Then Tim made a joke about the fact that eating off stone was probably even more primitive than eating oats and grain, and everyone could tell Kieran didn't want to say anything else and so they jumped on the bit, and in that moment, as it was taken away, Kieran realised he wanted nothing more than to tell these people everything that had happened and when and why and what it had cost him.

But they were laughing again, and the moment was gone, and they were toying with the idea of Steve Bannon as a kind of feudal lord, picturing the bitcoin farmers with their tinfoil hats in hand, stood in front of his digital throne, and Nina gave him a smile that was familiar, that meant you can tell me anything, or almost anything, but then it was gone, he had missed it, and so he kept the feeling, hoping to revisit it, knowing that it would be gone in the morning.

Outside night had fallen and the glass now reflected a faint image of the four of them. Kieran thought of the sad long head of the horse and wished he had touched it.

Ellie asked what Nina was going to cook when she hosted next and Nina said she was trying to eat seasonally, and Ellie said that actually the concept of seasons was quite Western and oppressive and even, dare she say, a little cowardly. Tim did an impression of a cowardly season, shrinking into himself and muttering about how he was unable to face all the buds and new life, and Kieran laughed so hard he slapped the table and made his cutlery jump, and did his own impression of a season begging for mercy from the other, bigger seasons, and that opened it up to the room.

And the space then filled with their moody seasons: nervous winter and naughty summer on a date, confused and lecherous spring, autumn that spent its time smoking clove cigarettes and drinking expensive coffee, and the concept of all of these pressed together, smothered and spread thin over the surface of the globe, arguing and competing, freezing and thawing and freezing again, needing each other, only existing in relation to the next.

Idolatry

Bonnie Lander Johnson

I

My daddy's a preacher. In a big broad square at the centre of Hackney is our church. With its red brick and sloping gables it's better than anything we had in Enugu. I don't remember that place except in my dreams but I've seen myself in pictures outside a mud-brick church. I'm a little girl in my mama's arms and we're surrounded by red dust and children. In those pictures my daddy wears white and smiles and smiles but nobody looks at him. They look at the camera instead, like it's the real miracle. Here in London no one's fooled by nothing and yet they know my daddy's a king.

We live in the house at the back of the church. High ceilings, low doors, a front room with a table long enough for fifty and a back room wide enough to hold the congregation. On Sunday after worship's done that room is jumping. We sing and play music and the women bring food, enough for us all to eat our fill and still carry bowls home. Plenty's what we have here. Plenty in our bellies and pockets and in the Spirit pouring onto us and there's no going back now.

Across the square are the Catholics. An old grey church filled mostly with Irish from the flats and gypsies from Wallis Road. But lately our people go there too. Nigerians and Tanzanians, Congolese and Somalis. There's enough of them now that they sometimes sing the Ave in Igbo. I don't know for sure because I never been but I heard about it. My daddy says they go there for the chanting and uchawi and sometimes they go there and still come here after for the worship and the party.

Our church and theirs stare across at each other day and night like birds of prey studying the field for kill. The square between us is a lawn of feeble grass, two benches and a few plane trees. It's kept by the council but not very well. That's why the Irish priest's come knocking. He says that his people and our people ought to care for that green ourselves and I know my daddy's thinking that none of his flock will sweat their bodies for a white man. But the Irish priest says over and over that it be Fellowship so my daddy can't say no.

It's almost spring now. The plane trees will soon be budding and the grass is beginning to sprout in mangy patches here and there. There are church folk, black and white, working in the square this morning, planting and seeding, raking and picking up rubbish. I watch them from the porch of our church because Daddy says that kind of work is not for me. But then they all start singing and I sing too from my place on the step. We sing some Catholic songs we all know, Aves and Jesus We Survive. And they follow along with our gospels in that way white people do, singing like they about to cry, not shouting their glory up to heaven. One white boy don't sing. I see him digging red flowers into the ground by the fence. He's wearing old jeans and a green jumper and his head is covered in hair pale as straw. He squints through his glasses so I can't see his eyes but his face is sweet.

At lunchtime my mama sends me over with juice and plates of chin chin and apples cut in slices. I am in the centre of the square with my sisters, holding trays of food. We are peacocks standing tall in dresses of blue, green, gold. The white boy comes up to me and puts the chin chin in his mouth. It's good. I know because my mama makes it. He looks up at me like he's never had anything so good in his mouth and he's smiling and eating some more. I don't know how to smile back at him. It's not anything I've seen my sisters do except when we're alone in the house. Outside we stand proud and serious like women to be respected. But I look back at that boy because his skin is so pale and I'm trying to see his eyes. Blue maybe, or green.

He's pushed aside by the movement of the crowd. I stand tall until my tray is empty. When I turn to walk back to the church he's still there near the tree watching me. I get a fear so my foot turns over and I'm on the ground. They all come to me then, lifting me and clicking their tongues and my mama shoos them away and takes me inside. My ankle's not hurt too bad, just tender. As we cross to the front door I turn and see that boy looking at me and I wish I'd kept myself steady for him.

II

The spring winds blow through the square and I'm sitting

outside on a bench under the plane trees for the first time in my life. That boy is sitting beside me and he's sneezing and sneezing into a handkerchief as big as a sail.

'Hay fever,' he says. 'You get it?'

'Never. We don't get that. We get asthma instead.'

'Do you have asthma?'

'Not me. I never been sick in my life.'

'Rubbish.'

'It's true,' I say, head high.

'You're like a princess.'

'No, I *am* a princess.'

That boy don't know if he should laugh. He's just looking at me doubtful until I smile and then he's laughing hard and sneezing again. He's got sweet pale skin on his face and neck, soft like cotton flowers, and his legs are long and thin. He sits with them crossed one over the other and his head hangs a little from his shoulders so all in all he don't take up much room on that bench. His daddy cleans the floors at the cloth factory and he's poor, poor, poor. I know my daddy won't like me being here with him but we're just sitting so there isn't anything he can say about it. That boy is lean and hungry but he's smart. He reads plenty. We've been here three days this week and he's fought it out with me over Dickens and now we're onto the Bible but that won't end well.

I say, 'We're really into the inspired passages, the ones about prophesying. Like "I will pour out my Spirit on all people. Your sons and daughters will dream dreams, your men will see visions."' I sit up straight when I say it with my eyes burning but he don't look too impressed.

'Oh yeah,' he says. 'That's good.' Then he just folds his

fingers together and looks out across at those red flowers
he planted. The new buds on the plane trees overhead are
ready to open their leaves. I can almost see them pushing
from the bark and into the warm air rushing round us. Now
and then a chill bites, winter fighting to keep its hold. But
there's no denying we're in the growing time. The apple
tree in my back garden wears pink and white blossoms so
beautiful and proud. I dance a little when I see it knowing
this is the year I'll turn seventeen and soon I'll be like those
apples, full blown.

I say, 'What's your favourite passage?'

He looks at me long and steady, eyes peering out
through his glasses. He's got a sweet low voice when he
says, "'Rise up, my love, my fair one, and come away. For
the winter is past, the rain is over and gone. The flowers
appear on the earth. The time of the singing of birds is
come, and the voice of the turtledove is heard in our land.
The fig tree puts forth her green figs, and the vine with the
tender grape gives sweet perfume. Arise, my love, my fair
one, and come away.'"

I don't know what to say. We just sit in silence for a
long time. Then I clear my throat and he jumps a little.

I say, 'You know all of that passage? Well enough to
teach me?'

He nods and nods but he don't look at me. He just
looks down at his fingers or out over the square.

That night in my bed I close my eyes and hear his voice
saying, 'Arise, my love, my fair one, and come away.'

Then I fall asleep and dream that I'm lying on the desert
floor under a tree I cannot name and my body is a flower
opening in the sun. He is near me but I can't see his face

and I think, Let him kiss me with the kiss of his mouth for thy love is better than wine. Wine runs over me in streams of red and he drinks from my cupped hands, from the bowl of my belly and the valley of my breasts. My skin is black from the sun, black and beautiful like the curtains he draws around us at night. The night sky falls in curtains around us, its stars golden points hollowed out and they look through the curtains at our love.

I wake just before dawn. My body is drenched and I'm breathing hard. The light outside the curtains is pale with the first flush of day, like sun shining down through deep river water. All that morning in the kitchen I watch my mama as she moves around making the food. She's tall and beautiful, her head bound in a bright-yellow gele tied high like the wings of a bird. I watch the way she carries herself, the movement of her spine, her chest full. I eat some melon and drink milk.

Back in my room I sit on the bed and see my own body beneath me. Long and young. I dress myself carefully like I'm treasure. That boy won't be coming today so all I have is the memory of his words and this is what he says to me: 'I am the rose of Sharon and the lily of the valleys. As the lily among thorns, so is my love among the daughters. As the apple tree among the trees of the wood, so is my beloved among the sons. O my dove, in the clefts of the rock, in the secret places let me see you.'

III

He says, 'So do you speak in tongues?'

We're on the bench under the plane tree and it's summer now. The light's pushing hard through the leaves. The grass is looking better this year now the church people done the seeding. It's dense and green and I think how good it would be to lie and feel the earth on my back and see the light peer through the leaves above. But there's no way I'm lying in the square or my daddy will never let me back here. I know he watches from the window but all we do is sit and talk so there's nothing he can say about it.

I say, 'My daddy sometimes speaks like that, full of the Spirit. And maybe one or two others. But not me. Why, your people don't do that?'

'Never. Unless you mean just speaking wisely. For us, that thing about Pentecost is a metaphor. We don't read it literally.'

'You say that all the time.'

'Well it's true. A lot of the Bible is a metaphor.'

'And how do you decide which bits aren't?'

'It's complicated.'

'Metaphor, complicated. Where you learn to speak like that? I know your school and they don't teach that.'

'No, they don't.'

His cheeks burn red and he looks out across the square. He don't like it when I tell him he's smart. I do know that school. I went there myself before Daddy raised enough to send me and my sisters to the big stone college where they're trying to make me speak right. I don't remember this boy from when I was at his school but that's because I never looked at the white boys then. I'd say that school is where he learnt to hang his head low so no one eyes him up for beating.

He knows his scripture well and on Sundays he and his daddy help the priest. I think he knows more than anyone else round here. I've been trying to read as much as him but he reads two books a week even though he cooks the food. His mother died when he was eleven, her body eaten through with cancer. Now all he and his daddy got to live on is the cleaning wage. They got a council flat behind the square so rent's not too high and the boy don't have to work himself. But he's busier than me round the house with the cooking and cleaning and he still finds time for reading. I got to the point now where every word I read – novels or poetry, it don't matter what it is – I'm thinking of him and what I'll say to him about it. But I don't tell no one about him, not even my sisters. What would I say?

Now it's almost summer holidays and I'm not sure what that means for us. I thought I'd ask him about that today and I wore my purple dress. When he saw me his face went red as an apple and he said I looked 'splendid'. He didn't say it in that old-fashioned way, like people say splendid when they just mean plain good. He said it like he meant the word properly, because that's my purple dress all right: like a royal bird. That's how I felt when I put it on this morning and that's how I felt when he said 'splendid'. But now we're sitting together and talking, I feel overdone.

I say, 'You mean your people never moved by the Spirit?'

'Oh sure. But not . . . Well, I suppose it depends what you mean by moved.'

'Inspired. Full of words and praise.'

'Yes, but we go inwards. We're full of feeling but quiet about it.'

I wonder what would happen to words when they're turned around inside a person like that before they come out. Like food cooked long and slow. And I say, 'I am come into my garden. I have gathered my myrrh. I have eaten my honeycomb and drunk wine with my milk. I rose up to my beloved. My hands dropped with spices and my fingers with sweet myrrh.'

He listens close, smiling deep into his collar. The afternoon creeps closer to evening and the square starts to fill with people drinking and talking loud. I say goodbye to him and walk back to my house. Only when I've eaten and washed and gone to bed do I say the rest of that passage to myself, out loud in the darkness of my room. 'My beloved is white and his head is the most fine gold. His cheeks are as a bed of spices, his lips like lilies, dropping sweet myrrh. His belly is as bright ivory and his legs are as pillars of marble. He is Lebanon, excellent as the cedars. This is my beloved and my friend, O daughters of Jerusalem.'

IV

Those plane trees hold onto their leaves longer than any other tree around here so that by the time they've covered the ground with gold we're well into the dark days. Then the low autumn sunset reaches its fingers through the buildings to light the gold that covers the square. For a moment just as we're closing up our church on Sunday London looks drenched in honey. It's getting harder to sit out on the bench now it's colder. That boy and I have maybe one hour to ourselves in the afternoon. We listen to the wind. This time of year it whispers and the dry leaves sing back to it. I say to him that winter's on its way and I see a sadness over that boy. He tells me it will soon be the Mass they say each November for his mother. I feel a fool for not knowing how he feels. No one in my house has died.

He says, 'I don't suppose you'd like to come?' And I get a pain inside me like I want to cry. But the feeling passes and I think that really all he's done is invite me to church. Then I remember that inside him he's hurting bad and I do what we never done in all the months we've been sitting here. I lift his hand from his lap and fold it inside mine. His fingers are long and cold.

I say, 'I'll be there.'

I don't have no black dress that fits me anymore so I make one. It's been two years since I took my measurements and now my chest and hips are the same inches as my mama but my waist is smaller than hers. I have some plain black cotton and I tally the inches like Mama taught me and cut the pieces crossways so it fits snug but not too snug. I tell my daddy that a kid from the old school has a memorial Mass and anyway now Daddy and the Irish priest are good friends he don't mind me going to that church so long as I don't start praying on beads. But I'm nervous going there on my own because who am I really? Just the daughter of the preacher. I'm not sure if that boy's daddy even knows my name.

The church is full and quiet. Candles burn everywhere and the organ is low and sad sounding. All the pews are full. Up the front is a whole row of priests, black and white, waiting at the altar to remember that lady. The boy and his daddy sit facing them and I feel a pain in me. Where else in this world do men so poor get respect like that? I don't know where to put myself. I stand in the aisle looking for any face I might know but there's none. Then I see that boy turn in his seat and look at me and he takes off his glasses so I can see what his eyes are saying and I follow to where he wants me.

All those months on that old bench we never sat this close but now we do because the pew is full. I can see both men been crying. His daddy looks old and worn out. But that boy – crying makes his face bright. There's a picture on the altar of his mother and she's smiling so wide I feel sorry she's gone. I look at that boy and his daddy and think it's not right for men to be alone like that. Then the priest begins to read, "'Oh that you were like my brother, nursed from my mother. If I found you outside, I would kiss you and no one would despise me. I would lead you into my mother's house. Come, my beloved, let's go into the field. Let's go early to the vineyards and see if the vine is in flower. There I will give you my love.'"

V

It's a sin to lie but I think right now it might be worse to not lie. The frost is heavy on the ground and no sane person would sit out on that bench all afternoon in the dark and cold just to talk. So I will lie to my daddy. But I've decided that it's all right because if I don't lie I will shut myself off from the Spirit that moves in me. Isn't my daddy always preaching that the gifts of the Spirit are joy and freedom, love and hope? And if I sit indoors all winter on my own I think that good Spirit will move on and I might die like a hollow tree.

The apple tree in our garden is bare as the plane trees out front. All around us is naked wood except the evil green on the yew with its brazen berries. This Sunday is a big day for worship and feasting and my family will be busy in the church for hours. I say I'm sick and I sneeze and sneeze and go to bed. Then when I hear the singing loud up in the rafters I slip out the back door and across the square to the grey church where he's waiting for me. The priest is doing hospital calls but that boy has a key from all his work in the sacristy.

I meet him at the back. He's wearing an old wool coat and has blankets under his arm. We go down the stairs and inside the hall he boils the kettle and gets teacups and plates from the big cupboard. I have a box of chin chin and we make a picnic on the floor. He folds the blankets so we have something to sit on and something to wrap round us. The tea he makes is strong and milky and my chin chin are sweet. There's sugar crystal on his lips. We're sitting close and talking about Christmas and the food we'll eat in our homes that day. We haven't held hands much or sat too close or nothing, just talked. But even so I say, 'I don't think my daddy would ever let me marry you.'

If he'd taken it badly, been hurt or angry, it might've been easier. Instead he just nods like he understands why that would be so. And I think I can't take any more of that boy feeling low in himself. So I put my mouth to his and taste the sugar and everything is sweet: his tongue and the way he folds his arms around my waist.

He says, 'I don't want to take anything from you if I can't marry you.' And I think I never wanted to give anything so bad.

I say, 'Let me be the boy and I'll take it from you.' He smiles and shakes his head and we kiss until we're breathing hard. I say, 'We could just lie down.' And we do. His body is warm. Through his clothes I hold him and his face is more golden than the summer or the first blush of blossom on the apple tree. Everything he taught me with his words is true. He's my fruit and my myrrh, my gold and honey, the milk of my love.

He's under me now and I feel a rush when he says my name. Then my mind is quiet as his body calls. I don't know much but I know my beloved is mine. He walks among the lilies. A garden of fountains, a well of living waters, flowing streams from Lebanon. Until the day is cool, and the shadows flee away, turn, my beloved, and be like a young deer on the mountains of Bether.

In the quiet of the church hall I say to that boy, 'I was asleep, but my heart is awake. It's the voice of my beloved who knocks. Open to me, my dove, my undefiled, for my hair is wet with dew and I am sick with love.'

Clara By Every Name

Hannah Retallick

My name is Clara and I'm not like other girls. I have been Janet, Gwendolyn, Katherine or Kathy, and every other name that my mother could form between a stranger's 'hello' and 'who's this lovely young lady then?' I answer to anything, with no more thought than if it were darlin' or hun. It's always been this way, ever since my mother saw the light, saw life for what it was, and withdrew. We travelled from place to place in her battered dark-blue van, foraged the hedgerows with nettle-stung hands and foraged the cities with her smiles, only spending money on essentials such as petrol, soap, paint, and black silk dresses.

We were in London for one cold winter, parked up on different side streets, never in the same place two nights running: too risky. No ID or driver's licence, but we would have been discovered in the end. *Found: middle-aged woman with young daughter, driving illegally. Help needed with identity. Is it . . . could it be them? The ones who disappeared all those years ago?* My mother was a professional shadow. The few times we were caught, her disguise held and she weaved her way out of trouble – I don't like to think about how; usually we weren't noticed at all. They had stopped looking. *Presumed dead?*

'Sweetie,' she'd say. 'If you look respectable, no one thinks to ask questions.'

I was nine years old and became Timothy, followed by Charlie, Michael, and Our Youngest Child Jeremy, but those were only during the weeks after the unfortunate 'professional' haircut, a backstreet job, £2 per child, a deal too glittery for my optimistic Father Figure to turn down. I was a boy, and I liked it at first, seeing how much more important it made me, how easily I could make my square jaw fit.

Its strength surged to my fists as I used them to show Bob Punter that I was indeed not like other girls. He was a boy a few years older than me who tried to take my cola-bottle sweets, thinking I was an easy victim, skinny and scraggy. I pushed him against a filthy dustbin and beat him around the head with our latest discarded number plate. His crying cuts begged for mercy.

Then my blond mop grew back, curving around my chin. I felt myself shrink, weaken, but not completely disappear. And then a new strength. I was a girl by the time we moved on again and have been ever since.

When I was twelve, we drove west through Devon and along the north coast of Cornwall. Angelica. That was the name I was given during the spring that Father Figure asked my mother an unexpected question. She said she would, but he didn't last long after that. Some things are better left unsaid. When Mother had met him, he was a stiff black suit, and she rescued him from the disease of modern society.

But he relapsed.

Angelica was a comfort to her then, with her powerful waves of empathy. Gentle and soft, nurturing, motherly, even as a twelve-year-old. I was Angelica for a long time to help her get over it, because she was heartbroken, you see, even though it was her decision – heartbroken that he wanted to stand still while she craved movement, that he wanted to be visible, burned into a lifelong contract, while she craved invisibility.

Mother took to sprawling on a big rock in a nameless cove – the same time every day, when and where he had asked – like a beached mermaid. It was the longest we were ever in a single place. She regretted that weakness but couldn't quite escape it.

On the last day we were there, she wore no coat even though it was a cold spring, and her skin was goose-bumped on her bare arms and upper chest. I returned to the van after a couple of hours of silent sitting. Using our camping stove, I warmed some sugary water, dipped in an overused teabag, and poured it into her red mug. As I crossed the rocks, trying to hold on to my notebook and the drink, I stumbled and sloshed tea into a shallow rock pool. I froze for a moment, transfixed by the cloud of milk that spread through the water and the ripples that eventually came to rest. How might that feel?

'Thank you, Jeremy. I mean, Angelica. Sorry,' said Mother. She took a lock of my growing fringe, sizing it up.

'Do you need anything else?' Angelica was a bit of a doormat really.

'You're writing?'

'Yes. I'm Charlotte, Mummy,' I said, daring to try a

different name, even if it wasn't the one I wanted.

She looked through me, then back to the sea. 'I suppose you'd better get on with it then, hadn't you?'

My bare feet became cold on the rock as I waited for goodness knows what.

Soon enough, she started naming me again. For the following two years I was Anne, Emily, Jane, Virginia, and as we travelled through northern England and into North Wales, I became Collette. Mother liked her spunkiness. Feisty and rebellious, this girl helped her mother steal a silver notebook from a Tesco in Llandudno, tearing off the barcode.

'Never the small shops,' said Mother. 'They're our people.'

Father Figure used to say that too, before he scarpered.

Mother and I cocooned in a forest in the mountains of Snowdonia. She cut my hair again but didn't make me a boy that time. I, Collette, perching on a fallen log, wrote furiously with the fountain pen Mother abracadabraed into my life. Collette needed it, and BAM! There it was.

Is Mother a witch? Is she a thief, like Collette? A demon? Or an angel with special powers? A fairy? These were the sort of questions I wrote in my notebook, questions I didn't want to ask her directly. And then there was the matter I could never discuss and was almost too scared to write. It stirred an increasingly strong desire within me. I wrote the answer instead:

Clara.

The name was a possibility, a distant memory, a word chanted internally; a name given and then taken, because it didn't seem enough. I found myself wondering, not for the first time in my life, whether I really existed. Or if I do exist, whether I am sentenced to be either formulaic or formless.

These thoughts blew away one day. My notebook disappeared. I never asked where it went.

We returned to Cornwall when I was fifteen. She scanned everywhere we drove and parked, as though looking for something she'd lost there – an engagement ring, perhaps. We hadn't heard from him since. How could we?

'No phones, Cleo,' she said, wearily. 'Nothing they could use to track us.'

Was it tiredness in her voice, or was it grief, yearning for what she's given up?

Missing: white woman, 33 years old, long black hair, with a bemused baby. Concerned for whereabouts. Please come home, darling, etc.

We flowed onwards because the thing she's looking for is no longer here. I knew she missed Father Figure because she still muttered his name in her sleep: Andrew, Andrew, Andrew . . . Where is he? After all these years, where?

I remember watching her profile as we hurtled round corners on bendy roads and hedged lanes, trying to see through the webby mane she'd chopped above her jawline as if to punish herself. But all I could see was the tip of a damp nose that could no longer sniff out the right path for us. Her back was hunched, unable to hold itself. This mystical Tinker Bell was killing herself with a different kind of poison: her growing, repellent stubbornness. *I don't believe in fairies. I don't believe in fairies. I don't believe in fairies. I don't, I don't.* My stomach churned and I looked ahead; it didn't help, because it wasn't just travel sickness, was it?

These fragmented reflections plucked from my life are where they belong: not immortalised in a glittery notebook but scrawled on a scrap of paper that's as transient as I am.

It is winter now, the middle of January, and I have just turned sixteen. Chasing warmth, we returned to London. It will be her final resting place. Some things are inescapable.

Mother has told me her story at least once a year; as if I could forget. Picture this: a powerful woman fills a crisp white shirt and black pencil skirt. She nearly drowns in ninety-hour weeks, and when her head breaks the surface for a moment, she gasps for breath, not caring what's in the air and inhaling anyway. Nine months later, a problem enters the world. There are no longer ninety hours in a week to work. That's when she escaped.

Sixteen years later, here she is, sick, with lumps on her breasts and a seeping nipple. She won't go to the doctor because she still refuses to exist. Ms Smith, Ms Carmichael, Ms Jenkins . . . they have no passports or NHS numbers.

It is a frosty Sunday. I have driven us to a side street, which is illegal given my age and lack of licence, but then my whole life has been illegal really, hasn't it? I wrap the red knitted shawl around her – it's decorated with random holes, dropped stiches, and tragic tea stains. I perch on the edge of the narrow bed, its softness caving a little and tilting her sidewards. I have become Ruth because she needs my care, a friend, a companion, not a daughter. I sleep curled up to her cold feet. She refuses all my food and drink offers, just shrinks. There's nothing more to say or do.

The most female thing that had ever walked the planet, everything that this world condemns and condones, is preparing for death in her classic black silk dress and the shawl of her making. If she had looked back to the beginning, she might have heard them say she'd had a breakdown and lost her mind. Alone, desperate and worked to the bone, she had been pulled left and right. They called for her whole being, every cell, every drop of blood. But what about me, The Problem? I screamed for her. I sucked my mother dry. My grandparents vampired her too. *You made your bed, you lie on it.*

The bed she has chosen now is a back-seat cradle. She's more trapped than ever, caught like a fish in an ice block. But she'll never change her mind, never admit that she's wrong, never give me what I need.

It's time.

I escape the claw fingers that plead with Janet, Gwendolyn, Katherine or Kathy, Ruth; with Timothy, Charlie, Michael, Our Youngest Child Jeremy; and with Charlotte, Anne, Emily, Jane, Virginia, Collette, Cleo and . . . Angelica.

'Angelica, please!' She's her last hope. 'Please, don't leave me.'

As I walk away and hear the cries from deep in her heaving chest, I imagine the message I would leave if we had phones: *I'm sorry, Mother, but Angelica cannot take your call. She doesn't exist. Beep.*

Instead, I turn, return to the open window next to her, and laser-scan her corpse-in-waiting.

'What do you want? Who are you calling?'

She can't or won't answer. I must leave. Given then taken; just like my notebook, she stole my name from me, stole the life I could have had.

My name is Clara and I'm not like other girls. I *am* the other girls. All of them, in one body, not formless but fluid. They can't make me choose.

Selling Oil

Shazia J. Altaf

There's a camaraderie around the team. There has to be. It pushes up sales. A flapping-over-paper board stands in between the humming processor screens and people, on skinny silvery legs, tallying their sales targets and trajectories by individual name, as they climb, suspend, or descend during the course of the week.

'She can sell oil to the Arabs . . .' laughs one of her colleagues, Phil, larking across the mossy-green desk dividers. Lofty thin teeth, and broad-backed. Clad in smart shirt, tie, and pressed trousers. They are in competition for sales. *Big hitter of the week*. Everyone is.

'*Car Insurance, how can I help you?*' A communal chorale of chatter, resonances rising in waves around banks of desks, weaving, feeding into cables on the call centre's open floor. The bitter smell of coffee grounds catapulting from throats. The usual, '*How many years no claims bonus? . . . What would you like your excess to be? . . . Any modifications? . . . You take care now . . . Blah blah blah . . .*'

She pivots off in her seat, the metal wheels rotating to

the neighbouring white-plastic windowsill, trying to filter out the bubble of pitching, fake, adrenaline-charged voices, even the repetitious drone of customers where possible.

Cable wires stretch their black coils allowing her some pull, some give, yet keeping her static. Gazing out across the landscape, at the dull, purpose-built cement bulks with flat rooftops, covered in reflective glass, standing their ground, rooted in the industrial park on the outskirts of town, at the sparse grass between offices, already yellowing like dead worms under the hardening sun. Failing to gauge any sign of limb or life inside at this nocturnal hour. The air con burrs above, suckling the air, streaming out mechanical blasts.

New modern-day factories. *Call a fucking centre.*

The foamy grey headset pads fasten to the ridges of her earlobes, the metal frames running inside resolutely, clinched by the cords, the snap of two clicks by her fingertips monitor her into the system. Toilet breaks noted, minutes, seconds recorded, somewhere out of sight reams of data collected, enumerated. *Should be grateful really.* This call centre was the crème de la crème of call centres. There were bonuses for a start. It'd help out Amma and Abba, a bit.

One place right in the town centre, on the old Corporation Road, she lasted barely half a day. That was because a threadbare-headed small guy, with extra-tight-fitting trousers, and his mirror associate paced around like a new breed of henchmen. Locking the stripping wooden doors, bolting them down, as they nervously rattled till lunchtime.

Ice-cold calling, ringing randomers. Lots of hoarse-frothing shouting through silver cavities, and nervy eyeballing of staff, as an incentive. When finally their combat-booted legs turned to the doors, and snapped the bolt necks down, she de-incentivised, did not return for dead phone lines, and vitriolic smacks by people who don't wish to be called. Preferring to stock shelves on night shifts like she had at her Christmas temp job. Missing the peace of the trolley, the empty aisles, no customers.

After the four-week training period, passing a series of assessments and 'technical' tests, she joined the Insurance team. A woman fiftyish, Maria told her cheerily that first week, 'Sex sells . . .' dipping knowing eyes. She learns later on, it's a slight touch, a deep pause, a huskier intimation, a subtle more *fuckable* tone, it's an emphasis on a word, the men, not all, some, are malleable.

'She's a dark horse she is. I've listened to her calls,' pipes in the team leader Eleanor, with a softly smirky gaze, when the team teases her good tally that week, a year in.

She was better with the men, a trick in the tongue, Maria was right, her sales proved as much. Exceeding let alone hitting the numbered targets as they whooshed past.

She got on the 184 bus after her last seminar of the day, Ancient Greece.

'. . . *but it always has been, is, and will be an ever-living fire* . . .' The lecturer, a drooping stump figure voicing Heraclitus to mostly zoned-out students. He had a dross voice beckoning the sleep chamber. Needing a black kava tea from Amma, the morning's energy boost flagging amidst the stale, burgeoning afternoon. Sad cavernous lines etched across Amma's forehead refocus her. Those lines weigh down her spine. Amma tells her about things far away, picking dead plants off graves' faces . . . A father, who died whilst Amma waddled her first clumpy steps, stolen lands, and a mother taken away not long after . . . A caged bird singing, ululating, a tear fiend. Those woes and others are viscous, congealing inside the chest cavity. She is happy to find the door and escape sometimes.

She checks behind the sticking zip. There's enough coins for bus fare and crisps later. Just. The stuck-in-the-1970s, beigey-grim bus depot was devoid of much custom. The sun was seething of late, showing you a different side to its face, creating a feeling you were not far from ash. Flopping into a furry seat as the bus lurches, sweat pools trickle down the nub of her back. A boy on the other side of the aisle admires a newly acquired pet hamster on his lap, mother atop his shoulder watching the run on the tiny feet, the nervous flickering pin-dot eyes, the hypnotic infinite wheel . . .

Cold anxiety spikes the base of her neck. The scaling traffic curls a tail around the bus. Her shift started at 5 p.m., less than fifteen minutes left, she can't be late, but she wasn't going to make it either. In front, a man with rimless glasses scrapes silver paint incessantly from a stack of lottery scratch cards. *What sense was there one person winning three hundred million or whatever, or one person having bazillions . . . ?*

Off the bus her skin singes under the sharp light, the heat leans heavily on her shoulders, the boiling concrete grasping through papery leather sandals to the soles of her feet.

The floor manager, a mouse-like woman, hair scraped

back, tiny dot eyes moving everywhere, surveyed things by the entrance door. Keeping her head down meekly, she remembers post wisdom teeth extraction last month, blood draining, oozing trails on her pillow refusing to clot to stop, she took one day off for the engorgement. The floor manager pulled her up, by way of hello . . . leading to the absence for the abscess.

'People normally still come to work you know . . .'

The taste of blood, iron still on her tongue. The job is to talk, smiling dumbly, saying nothing outwardly, remaining teeth-tight, good naturedly, as she ought, as she must, as she will.

There is a copy of *American Psycho* on Mark's desk, who normally sits to her left. He flicks in and out of it, unsure whether genuinely liking it or trying to appear edgy. His face has a deceptive permanent scowl, rapping fingers on his ripped jeans, a fading tattoo resides on the inside of his index finger.

There's a new girl that has started, a real-life Barbie. Symmetrical face. Fake eyelashes, matching imported silicone blobs to go. Lashed in dark fake tan that looks like it has not been rubbed into the skin properly, refusing to absorb.

Scavenging together the copper and silver to feed the vending-machine slit on break, she heads downstairs for Thai sweet chilli crisps. Having no chance for any tea. Running on the diddy tuna mayonnaise bap she managed to wrangle from the uni café queue. Hunger crawls inside her entrails. Many hours left till home. Amma was over the flames, back turned stirring pots of lady's fingers, black-eyed beans, and halwa when she flew out the door, rucksack flapping. Her lips whetting at the caramel-sandy thought.

There'd been a fifty-pence coin by the windowsill in her bedroom, but a bug lay dried out on its back, legs mid squirm in the air making her forget to pick it up, it seemed kind of wrong.

In the staff kitchen, a neighbouring team leader leans by the side of the fridge slopping cold cottage cheese out of a white pot, trying to make sure curdled crumbs are not left on her thin lips.

She clicks open the fridge to get some milk for tea, normally all that keeps her going during shifts. Sad sandwiches drooped sunken under the weight of clingfilm, pots of watery soup, bruised spotting bananas, blue veins clawing cheese, mouldy not matured, making her stomach turn, the milk bottle sloshing going past them, she spills a few drops into her cup, quickly replacing it back, as if she didn't pay the required pound towards the communal milk kitty.

Offering peace of mind to policyholders . . .

It's QA this week. Quality Assessment. They do 'random' remote checks in a tiny glass box in a corner off the top floor. She imagines the quality-control checkers wading knee deep through reams of calls, suspended on circular disks, pulling the film tapes back and forth, listening in, pausing, rewinding the rotational disks, going back in time, as they eavesdrop. Her best friend Khadijah, who works at a tentacled call centre in the town dealing with mobile contracts, says she regularly cuts off the customers. *The ones who are being twats.* Cuts them dead right there on the phone line. She wishes sometimes she could do the same. They mustn't have the same glass box they do here.

At the triangular desks, ten are wedged tightly to form a circle, she picks up the spindly metal frame tunnelling her back to the merry-go-round of accents, tones, and never-ending annoying querying voices.

'Are you going to the do?' says Phil, long legs confidently apart, seated two chairs down the left, averting his eyes back to the keyboard typing. His half-moon face under a freckly net.

'Yeah, think so . . .' She nods at him, hopeful. She'll have to sneak out, it should be fine.

He nods back then grins. It's becoming an unsaid thing between them. The waiting looks, meek glances, averting, reverting eyes. *Pointless though . . .*

The annual celebration do, a posh do, a black-tie affair at the Draythorne Hotel, everyone's excited, extra chirp lacing tongues. A free meal on the company tab.

Maria's lipstick has veered off into the corners of her mouth, threatening a slight clownish look, like that creepy one lying in wait under the road drain in that horror movie. 'Was watching an Indian documentary last night, don't mind me saying this . . .'

Her mind groans.

'Is it all mud huts out there? It's just what you see on the TV . . .' Her voice earthy, salty, lowering on the last sentence, as if her voice box knows it is off. The words slip off, like they've been waiting to come out the back of her throat for a while. Lipstick spreading like grease.

A trio of pigeons she spies through the window are shitting, dive-bombing dropping their loads outside.

She wants to tell her about ancient gateways, the daunting pillars guarding the entrance to the elevated, diaphanous-glazed house with scalloped jalis, latticework rising along cantilevered balconies laying the moon in your lap. Impressed ancient stones and deodars, glassy marble moulded by old Kashmiri hands from old Kashmiri times, secrets in their nails in their graves . . . She guesses here would sell for more than Maria's entire Next-laden house. But she doesn't say anything, they will only think she is lying.

'It's like any country where there's money there's more comfort, I guess . . .'

'Talha is like some descendant Asian princess, I bet,' Phil says.

'Yeah, nah, wouldn't go that far.' She laughs, the temperature rising pinching at her cheeks.

'Hate bourbons they're like dirty cheap . . . biscuits,' Barbie says randomly, as if from nowhere, or from a conversation she was having with someone else, but did not seem to be, or one in her head. She glances between the guys and then back to her, then back to the guys awaiting a response. A touch stiffly, the voice accusatory, whilst declarative.

So, these silly games.

'I kinda like them . . . Hit the spot,' answers Mark's scratchy voice behind his pod without moving his head. Barbie throws a surly glare and goes back to the call queues, flicking a curtain of other people's hair stuck to her scalp. Barbie is looking for a Ken. Mark, she senses, is the

Ken she chooses, wishes to mould, but Phil would also do.

Whispers creep bouncing off pristine-white-walled corridors. There has been a customer complaint. A customer claims they were not told about the ultra-high excess on a policy they were sold yesterday evening. And they claim they were cut off too quickly when they questioned this. Their call will have to be trawled, and checked back by the quality controllers. Everyone hates this, and no one knows yet, who has been complained about. The axe falls for any misdemeanours. Nothing will be discovered until the investigation has been carried out inside the translucent glass box nobody can see.

* * * * *

She has been off sick a couple of times in the last year, once with a tummy upset, a viral vomiting shitting both ends affair, once a bad head flu, coupled with her recent back-teeth-out off day, has triggered a meeting for her slightly higher than average 'sickness rate'.

The neighbouring team leader in the corridor before the said meeting says, 'It's up to you what happens,' smiling corporately, cryptically.

'Why do you think your sickness is high?'

An HR woman she has never met or seen before conducts the meeting. Trepidation flutters on her lips. She jokes she isn't a serial sicker, nerves jangling like keys she doesn't know the locks to. The woman's fountain pen jerks to stop writing, she gazes awkwardly, assessing her, she knows straightaway, she has said the wrong thing, as if she has said, she is a serial killer. *What an idiot!* She needs this job badly to get through uni, and for Amma's eyes and pearly tears.

'*You will be notified about our decision for action in due course . . .*'

She dreams strange dreams, machines with wires needled through mouths on pulley systems . . . neck, chest, and the coiling spine down between her thighs all soaking wet when she wakes . . .

* * * * *

Optional extras?

Quickly ducking into the patiently waiting taxi, so Dad doesn't see the black plastered top, he's funny about full arms and bare shoulders being out and about. She had made an effort, dressed in a silken long black skirt. She hadn't managed to find the right top to match in the shops. In a stroke of genius, because she knew the effect she wanted, spying one of her mother's black chiffon scarves to wrap, layer her silhouette. It matched the silk skirt perfectly. Laiqa, her sister, cocooned the material around her, placing safety pins inside near her breastbone, as she told her to, pin to bone, mummifying her chest. Hair strands loosely tossed up with black hair grips slicing into the head, a black, flowing, cloudy plume. She thinks she sees Dad's face flickering behind the upstairs window, but she can't be sure . . .

The dinner is a bag of shite. The vegetarian option is a

steamed sagging cauliflower head, streaked with a few dead herbs, assumed to be haute cuisine. The others crush rare steaks and roasted potatoes against teeth, the pink almost bleeding onto enamel. Luckily, she has already eaten some chicken karahi before she left for the do. She knows the score with these things, these places.

Her mother is in one of her moods, as she leaves the house. The fringed, triangular shawl out of sorts. She humours her to make it easier to leave. She nearly slips on a rain-soaked condom getting in the taxi leaving their dark neighbourhood. She blames Amma for getting her flustered, for not seeing it and being alert as she normally is. Pennies and pounds can't always be found. *Nothing fucking new there.*

Amma has the Kashmiri gift of slicing to the bone with a twinkling glint, leaving you trouserless. There are thieves cloaked as those close, Amma remembers, and talks of, she cannot get at these living spectres, who rejoice having stolen what is hers, the map in her body has not forgotten, what has been withheld, what she is owed . . . She's the keeper of stories . . . but far away in England, it is almost impossible. Sacrificial face. Gripping the wooden spoon stirring the lady's fingers, catching them before they burn, Amma says in Punjabi slang, 'Go ahead eat, eat it . . . It'll come out in this world or the next . . .' She says it like an ancient curse to invisible alive phantoms, it's an innocent proverb, yet on her tongue it could easily be a knife.

Barbie's wearing an LBD, a little black dress, to deliver a knockout blow. They were both in pitch jet black. She smiles at her, Barbie serves it back bristling. Unverified whispers transmit between maws and bent-back palms naming Barbie as the complained-about individual, but nothing as of yet has been confirmed. It could be anyone.

People start to dance, the base pumps permeating, pulsating in her chest. A sea of limbs takes on strange convoluted shapes attempting routines. New Order come on after a lot of crap dance tracks set on an almost endless loop. This is the song. Heady chords let you through veiled blue fields . . . She's enjoying herself . . . She can feel eyes on her, Phil stopping on the tip of her nose, the net of his freckles opening, they've been dancing on the edges for a while now . . .

After the meal people scuttle into known hubs, the drinks gush, dripping sickly, stickily. There's a company tab to take advantage of. Not for her, she is teetotal as a Muslim. How many Cokes can she drink, not many. A black liquid glass crackling ice in her palm, she shakes the bobbing cubes, sipping soda bubbles, watching the melee of black ties and gaping tits.

Phil comes over. Barbie appears like a magnet, joining them, seemingly blanking her. Hair yanked in a ponytail grip, makes you think of kids trailing plastic dolls, holes in their heads where they've previously pulled fistfuls of nylon tresses out of their scalps. Bad vibes ooze underneath a perfectly contoured mask. Mark joins. Jokes, laughing, dancing, liqueurs lacquering throats, dagger eyes crawling out of fake eyelash legs. Ostracised subtly in a four-way conversation one way.

'I'd rather have her . . .' Touching his chin Phil pointing to her, having downed a few pints already, becoming inebriated. She doesn't know how they have come to this. Cattle livestock at a farmers' market. She laughs it off.

Barbie has to rearrange her face. Rattled, sweat molecules rise in the cakey make-up bloom. Teeth bleached eerily white. Each feature disjointed, surprised at the outburst, and trying to align back with visible difficulty. The shimmer, the mascara, the lipstick, the blusher, all stood on end for a split second, separating before coming back down to the base of her face. Fault lines unsettled in the ground.

'You two want her on a spit roast,' Barbie says, there's a hiss in her saccharine voice only she can hear. They giggle, ignoring her.

She knows it wasn't a compliment, she will have to look it up online, as she doesn't know what a spit roast means. Barbie flounces off, pissed off.

Opulent rooms dripping decadent walls, strolling through trailing verdant gardens drenched in glittering lights. Thumbprints on hourglasses. The night wears in darker, muskier, the people become worse for wear, loose, sloppy, getting soused. Introverts flip, and vice versa, making plans to do things . . . not knowing what they've said or done, and to whom . . . Base notes of desperation deepen like fog. Beyond here long-term commitments and vows are broken wide open, sharply.

Phil tries to tuck a slip of her hair away from her face. 'Maybe we could meet up away from here . . . and see how it goes you know . . .' he says, sadly hopeful.

No, she doesn't know.

He strokes her ear, which feels a little weird, and she

tries to move away, shaking her head. 'I love her . . . but I'm not in love with her . . .' Phil says of his girlfriend, but she isn't in the business of taking other girls' men. She smiles, touching the winglike blade popping out of her back, stares at the ground, nods, and moves away. A vanishing act.

* * * * *

Heading for the toilets quickly before the weekend's morning shift, she encounters Barbie's outline by the basin, talking on her mobile to a friend it sounded like. Momentarily Barbie flashes steel-blue eyes, and carries on chatting.

She pisses, as quietly as she can feeling rude whilst someone is talking on the phone right outside the suspended cubicle door, weakening her piss sound, hoping it won't be transported through airwaves. Rinsing her hands quietly, she hears an old familiar vile term, it rhymes with 'khaki' . . .

Tongue stripped, coldly sliced. Calmly, she pulls a paper towel, without looking, carries on walking, open-mouth shock, surprise jutting her hip bones along.

Why didn't she say anything? she scolds herself.

They are not in competition, there is no competition that she can see. Looking down, a yellow hoodie, fraying navy baggy pants, a bushy head against a glamazon, as if. *Funny, how she wants to look like a khaki though . . .* brown cream dolloped on in fat splodges on the daily, in a colour that could rival her great-daadi-ma, who had been out in the Kashmiri sun her whole entire life. She must think, as soon as the brown eyes are here, it's over for the blue-eyed bitches. She stretches her fingers, pulls them back one by one to hear them crack over the keyboard.

The windows draw in the northern sky, yellowing-grey light overhanging the desk, catching the ratty jacket of *Catch-22*. She left Yossarian pointlessly trying to get out of flying again. The seconds crawl on their backs. She gulps down cold tea. She thinks of her mum's tea, cardamom and star anise waterlogged in a milk pan; she could do with its thick balm embalming her. Barbie returns to her desk, as if nothing has happened, unfazed and unbothered.

Acting like her shit don't stink.

The voices swirl . . . The roof of her mouth is bone dry, catching her tongue. The blood rising in her cheeks like slapped skin. The weight of *the word* slackens her jaw. The paracetamols she took before the shift for an achy head, the chalky tablets nearly got stuck, constricting, refusing to go down the oesophagus's tunnel. Something is rising, she needs to keep it down.

She tries to loosen the wires wrapping her carefully. A toe dipped in each world, a call-a-gob job approaching like a bullet train once uni finished, barrister dreaming slithering from her reach even as she's grasping . . . *There were no jobs . . . She's living in cloud cuckoo land . . .* Loads with degrees in here. IT degrees, business degrees . . . countless others with their lips to the wire. She swivels in her seat to the window ledge. She must subdue the rise in her ribcage, the sinking, dragging pull.

Someone turns up the TV, the screen pops alive, as if startled from the usual drudgery of daytime soaps and cosy doctor and crime serials, the transmission feeds bizarre images . . . smoking plumes, fireballs rising out of giant buildings . . . planes . . . The air quietened.

. . . but it always has been, is, and will be an ever-living fire . . .

Her eyes want to check if what they see is real . . .

One woman on another team starts spluttering, rolling in her chair away from her desk, voice splintering, and thinks she sees something flying in the distance in the eerie grey-white near their window . . . Mouth loose, face wobbling in crawling slow motion. Gravity interrupted.

Her own brain has not left to jump to that realm of unreality that quickly. A wet prickling grows on her skin. The absorption of melanin identifying her. Gnawing discomfort twists and picks. New eyes look at her, pinching eyes . . . Or was she imagining it? Her veins, they tighten. She dry swallows, as her throat catches on itself.

What has begun . . . what will begin . . .

She returns to the padded seat and wonders how long she will be stuck. Head reeling . . . The unearthly TV images . . . black burnings . . . The long cast shadows will be permanent . . . she will stay here until wire and mouth meld as one . . . she will turn into a brown version of Maria selling sexy insurance, spitting odd lies in gaps, whilst the underwriters find ways to default . . .

She sees Amma in her mind at home with a split pomegranate on a rattan changair, the bloody seed sacs waiting to stick in your teeth . . .

Wet sheens her skin, ears seal with chattering tongues, the view sinks, the hours mount, neck tightening like a wrung rope. She needs to bury it. Voices like a deluge fill her lungs . . . She wants to speak to scream.

The call signal comes through jolting her.

The Rock

Miki Lentin

Come on, come on, answer, I mouthed. Hello, Maxol
Station, Swords Road, a voice said. Hi there. I . . . ehhh . . .
was wondering if you could help me. Yeah? I'm looking for
a rock. A what? A rock. We left it by the hoover machine.
When? Yesterday. Can you have a look and see if it's still
there please? I'll have to speak to the manager. Is he there?
He's on his break. It's white. What is? The rock. It's the
size of a mini rugby ball, and it's quartz. OK, can you call
back later?

The day before.
 You have to get rid of the rock, I said. What? you asked.
That's not what you said earlier. I did. I said that we'd have
to lose it before we got to the airport. There's no way we'll
get a rock that size past security, OK? No you didn't. You
said that you'd check online to see what's allowed on board
and what's not allowed and obviously you haven't done
that, as you never do what you say you're going to do. And
now I feel like a bad parent, the worst, because I haven't
checked online. What would I even look up? Can you take

a rock on board a plane? Well, it's too late now, I said, I have to finish cleaning the sand from the car and fill up and we still have to drive 2K to the airport and it's already half past. We have to go. It's not my fault we're running late. I didn't say it was. Well, why are you still cleaning the car? So we don't get fined. Look, it says it there. Drivers who return cars with sand in them will be fined 100 euro. All I said was that you have to get rid of the bloody rock.

I stooped down, my head now buried under the steering wheel filling with blood, the grooved tube of the petrol station hoover zipping against the car door, and vacuumed the fuzzy carpet, watching specks of sand bounce around like tiny comets. Briefly, I came up for air and saw you gripping the rock into your belly, covered by both sides of my cardigan that you were wearing, holding the rock like a toy bear, and saw your now teenage eyes well up with bubbles of hot tears, and your face swell like you've done since you were a baby, and that familiar sniffle that I know so well returned, and you reached into your pocket for a scrap of tissue that you used to dry your nose, which you always do rather than blow, the rock still in one hand, wiping the other hand on your brown cords, leaving a glisten of snot like a snail's trail on the ribbed material.

Where will I put it then? you asked. I don't know, I said. There, in that bin. You can't put a rock in a bin. Anyway, I'm not leaving Rock. It's mine. Mine, mine, mine. I don't care what you say. Rock now had a name. I don't know, put it there, by the wall, that way someone else can enjoy it. What? Do you expect someone to just find it? No, I'm not leaving it. Just leave it, come on, we can't take it with us. Well, what do you want me to do? You haven't told me what you want me to do.

You always ask me that same question when my instructions are unclear, perhaps because I'm not sure myself. All I knew was that we had to go. The last thing I needed now was an argument with you, about a rock.

And then I heard it drop. It wasn't a thud or a crack, more a cushioned landing, a stone falling on grass. I looked up from vacuuming, the blood returning to my body, and saw it lying on the ground next to the hoover machine, alongside an empty crisp packet. I hadn't noticed before, but sitting on the wall of the Maxol petrol station on the Swords Road, Dublin, next to the hoover, was an elderly man, just letting the world go by, oblivious to our fight. He was gaunt, almost deathly, shaving cuts on his face. He seemed drained, as if he'd walked for miles and wanted to sit down, somewhere, anywhere. The chipped breeze-block wall of the garage seemed as good a place as any, as buses and lorries belched past on their way to the airport that we needed to get to. What was he doing there? He seemed like a permanent living sculpture of the garage, something that would still be there if we came back the next day. He just sat, staring at the rock that you had dropped by his feet, next to the hoover.

Looking at the rock that time, I could almost feel your hands leaving it, that tingle of warmth on your fingertips from grasping its edges, the sharpness cutting into your palms leaving purple blood-filled indentations.

Get in, I said, we have to go.

You wrapped my cardigan around your body and slammed the car door. I brushed some sand off the passenger seat. A knock on the window. Hey, you can't leave that thing there, I heard someone shout. Jesus, who's that? I asked. Hey! Hey! The voice again. Open the window, you said. But we need to – The window whooshed open. What? I mean, yes? You can't leave that rock there, the station attendant said. Why? We can't throw it away. Sorry, we . . . have to go, flight to catch. But mister . . . I started the engine, turned my head, reversed, your hands gripping the seat. Bye, I shouted, beeped the horn and waved. We rejoined the traffic on the Swords Road. Your eyes met mine in the rear-view mirror. You always sit in the back. There was silence. Cold as ice. A taut expression on your face. Then you said, You're so embarrassing, do you know that?

A few days before.

I said we were going for a walk. I had to get out of the hotel. The air inside was dry, constricting. Reluctant at first, but then you dropped your headphones onto your Mac which you left open on your unmade bed, socks and T-shirts and books and used tissues scattered on the floor.

We drove. You and me out from Clifden in County Galway towards the coast. I wanted to walk on a beach. One of those beaches where even on grey days the light seemed to go on for miles and pierce my eyes. The villages became smaller and buildings more scattered as we drove on, until the road narrowed to a lane wide enough for just one car and jungly ferns, fuchsias, arrow grass and wild orchids brushed against the car doors. There was moisture in the air. A salty wetness. Damp, sticky, dripping.

Where are we going? you asked. I'm looking for a beach my father took me to when I was a kid. He used to like walking there when we came here on holiday. It's somewhere around here. But we can't swim, we didn't bring towels, you said. Well, I might dip my toes.

Thirty years on, the beach now flickered in my mind like a Super 8 film. We'd followed a handwritten sign with *trá*, beach in Irish, painted on it down a lane and found a sliver of dazzling white sand, see-through water, pebbles like eyeballs, jellyfish stuck to the shore. It's where my father and I dug a ram's skull out of the sand, where we washed it, where we laughed as seawater gushed out of its eye sockets. I asked if I could take it. At first he said no one would mind, but then said that we should leave it where we found it. It was better that way, he said, better to keep things where they belong. And yet I wanted it so badly. I wanted to feel the grittiness of the sand under my nails, snap the honeycomb bone tissue with my fingers, feel the smooth horns in my palms.

Before we walked, I wanted to drive across to Omey Island along the unnamed road, an expanse of sand that at low tide becomes a road of a few hundred metres. I thought it would be fun. You said that the car might get stuck in quicksand halfway, so we decided to walk. Ahead of us I could see a few rusty road signs tangled with seaweed embedded in the sand. Each one had white arrows on blue circular signs pointing forwards and backwards from either side, as if we needed reminding that whichever direction we faced, we are always going forwards and backwards.

As we walked you kept looking round at the car, wondering if we'd get back in time. I'm going back, you said. It's not safe. I can already see the tide coming in. Why is that person running? I'm cold. It's fine, I said. Look, the app says that we've got hours before we have to get back.

111

But why is he running? He's a jogger. Come on, when do you get to walk to an island like this? I'm going back.

You shot a road sign with your phone, turned and stomped your way back across the sand, retracing your footprints, placing your shoes into the same indentation that you made on the way out, so it showed you going forwards and backwards, footprints that would soon be swept away by the tide. Ten minutes later I got to Omey Island and looked back. I could just about make you out, your black hoodie under my cardigan up over your head, a shadow against the white hire car as drizzle danced in the air. Some sun was trying to poke through the clouds but failing. You prefer it that way.

What did I expect, as I looked at you hundreds of metres away? For you to love these far-flung places on the edge of nothing? I was doing that parental thing of trying to get you to like something that you had no connection to, but I wanted you to connect to. This could be the last time I would come to this part of the world. My mother, who lives in Dublin, is moving to Australia soon, so I'll have less reason to come to Ireland. We used to holiday here when I was young, the sun prickling our necks on our walks before we returned to a B&B, and then a meal of mussels and chips, the midges biting our bare backs as we slept. I still wanted to find the same beach nearby where we used to walk, where I found the ram's skull, where I used to skim stones with my father, where I'd curl up in a sandy towel after a dip in the icy water. I wanted to see this part of the world one last time. I wanted you to breathe it as much as I had to.

*

Empty your pockets please, an airport security guard said. Laptops in their own tray. Toiletries in a plastic bag. You emptied your pockets. One stone, then another, then another, then another. I counted sixteen: agate, basalt, conglomerate, granite, slate, rhyolite, quartzite, round, flat, oblong, pear shaped, pink, white, black, silver, blue, jade green, lime sea glass, all polished by the lick of the tide.

I thought I . . . What? Didn't I . . . You didn't say I couldn't take these. It was a pointless argument. You see. What? They didn't confiscate them. They didn't even look at them. You shoved me, your pockets now heavy again. I could have taken Rock.

But I also felt heavy, as if we'd left something behind.

We drove on. We were lost, trying to search for the beach. Every lane we went down with handwritten signs for *trá* all seemed to be dead ends or driveways to empty holiday bungalows, pebbledash walls and windows reflecting the watery sky. I know you don't like not knowing where we are going, so you asked where we were going every few minutes, as if I knew. A beach, I said. I'll recognise it when I see it. For some reason though, at that moment I didn't mind that we were lost. Amidst the muggy air and lichen-stained rock, I felt that we could just drive and drive and not worry about where we'd end up and you might enjoy that. At least that is what I hoped. I wanted to tell you that sometimes my mind is a black hole and I need a rope to climb out, but getting lost felt calming, freeing. We'd eventually find the beach, a beach, any beach, somewhere where we could walk.

It was close to three that afternoon when we came

across a beach near the town of Renvyle. The car was now musky with the smell of bodies, and you told me that I had promised a walk, otherwise you wouldn't have come, that you had better things to do. When I asked what those better things were, you didn't say. Come on, we're stopping here. There's a beach. Is this the one? you asked. I don't think so, but it looks beautiful.

I stepped on a length of barbed wire attached to a rickety fence with my boots so you could climb over, and we walked onto a sand dune through clumps of marram grass that scratched against our legs and down onto a beach that curved into the distance. Mackerel sky. The only sound a distant bark of a dog. The sun dead ahead of us now, still high on the horizon, lighting up our faces, glowing onto rocks that dotted the sand still wet from the tide.

You asked again if this was the beach I wanted to visit. No, I didn't think so, but it didn't matter. It was lovely anyway, and my father would probably have laid down here and let the waterlogged sand dampen his trousers and bald head, and he would have breathed.

You stopped amidst a jumble of seaweed, clumps of bulbous jelly-like roots left to dry on the sand. I looked at you from above, your eyes scrunched up behind your glasses against the sun, your hands knotted in a cat's cradle, your knees bent, and at that moment I wanted to apologise for all the things that I might not know about you, but I didn't. You just being here, with me, was enough.

I skimmed some stones, feeling the flattest ones I could find with my thumb and forefinger. They go further if they're flatter, I remember my father telling me. You tried to skim. The stones plopped into the still water in front of you. We laughed. I held your hand in mine. We both stooped forward. Our knees bent. Look into the distance, I said. Throw it like a frisbee. I can't, you said. Here, you do it. We breathed. Together. And skimmed. The first skim some feet away, the second and third in quick succession, the fourth a mere ripple into the waves. Yes, you said. I smiled. You see.

You started to gather rocks. Can I take these? you asked. Sure, I said. Are you sure it's not illegal to take rocks from a beach? I'm sure I read somewhere that it's illegal. Is it illegal? Will we be put in jail if we get caught? What? Who's going to catch us? But at the airport . . . Don't worry about that, I said. Why would they care? It's only a few rocks. Look, there's millions of them, millions. You smiled.

We compared stones and shells as we gathered, discarding the ones we didn't like, throwing them against other stones and pocketing the bright ones, the colourful ones, the fossils, rubbing the sand off on our trousers. It was then that you saw Rock.

It jutted up through the sand, as if it had been placed in that spot as a marker. Using your fingers you dug around the edges, sand trapping under your chipped fingernails, and pulled the rock out. White pristine quartz, with veins of earthy colours running through it like deltas of rivers, the lines on the palm of a hand. Polished and beaten by millennia of sand, seawater, wind and rain, it was perfectly smooth in places, rough in others. It somehow seemed to fit into both of your hands, large enough for you to hold, as if it wanted to be held, your hands able to mould themselves around the curves of the rock that had been blasted from something, a lost piece of glacial debris. You held it up to your ear, like a shell. What can you hear? I asked. The sea, you said.

We washed the rock in the sea, our bare feet freezing, trousers rolled up, our bums getting wet from the lapping waves, until the rock shone, translucent, a glowing white. You rubbed it dry with my cardigan and held it to your belly, not wanting to let it go, the rest of the rocks jangling in your trousers.

For a while we sat on the sand dunes and looked out. Dark rocks dotted the sea, tiny forgotten islands. The sun a whisper of light. You took out your phone and snapped.

You see, you said. What? I asked. I told you. What? I could have taken Rock. Here, I looked it up. There's nothing that says you can't take rocks on a plane. Thirty-four thousand feet up, this was the last conversation I wanted to have. OK, I mumbled. Sometimes I get things wrong. Sometimes. You put your earbuds back into your ears and pressed Play on your mobile. I looked away. Truth be told, I'd also wanted to take Rock with us, but sometimes I don't think, and it's easier to say no to a request than say yes, as if saying yes might be more freeing and remove some kind of constriction, but I enjoy that constriction sometimes, it keeps me on edge, makes me feel that I'm in control, an edge that sometimes is hard to fall away from. So I said no. Parental choice.

Dublin, my mother's apartment, the day before we flew back to London. I wanted to go for a drive. I had an urge to drive along roads and see places that I hadn't been to since I was a teenager – the garage wall where I smoked dope, the park where we threw batteries into bonfires while legging it, the hotel owned by my friend's dad where he served us apple pie and vanilla ice cream in the bar like hotel guests. I had an urge to be alone, but when I told you that I was going out, you said you wanted to come as it was too early to go to bed, and you weren't a kid anymore and you also wanted to see these places and I always did things alone, so how about it?

The night was clear, T-shirt warm. I opened the windows and let a breeze tickle my face. You edged your head out of the passenger window, the air flicking your hair. Led Zep on the stereo.

In truth there wasn't much to see. An apartment block had been built on the park, the hotel was gone, the garage a Londis or some such. Why don't you stop, walk around? you asked. I ignored you for some reason. Easier to say nothing than make an excuse, like there was nowhere to park. Truth was I didn't want to stop. I had spent the last few days creating images in my mind of all these places, like the beach I'd wanted to visit, and it seemed easier for the images to stay there. They were ruined by what I'd seen, fuzzy, blurred, and I was afraid that what I'd be left with was not what I wanted to see.

We drove on. Through the suburb of Kimmage, past where the Classic Cinema had been, the old age home where my grandmother died, around Harold's Cross Park, right and then left onto Leinster Road.

What are you doing? you asked. What do you mean? I said. We're going home. But, this isn't . . . this isn't . . . What? I asked, as I pulled over to the left outside number 88. This isn't your house, where Granny lives anymore, you said. I closed my eyes. I couldn't understand how it had happened. I'd driven to our old house, unconsciously, without thinking, as if I was drifting along the streets of my childhood, oblivious to what I was doing. But we are home, is what I wanted to say. I didn't. I closed the windows of the car and wanted to hide.

From the outside the house was dark, the grass in the front garden overgrown, the paint on the windowsills peeling, the lavender bed skeleton bare, the door painted red, gloss.

Come on, you said. Let's take a look. What? I asked. We can't. What if they see us? Who's they? I dunno, the new owners or something. We can't just poke about in the middle of the night. They'll think it's weird and I can't be arsed to make excuses. Yeah, do you mind us having a look? Yeah, I used to live here. No, you go. I'm not going alone. And then you grabbed my hand, and I realised that you hadn't looked for my hand like that since you were much younger. It's just not something that you do anymore, and it sent a ripple through me, as if it kind of woke me. We'll only be a sec, come on, don't be so boring.

We got out of the car and walked up the garden path to the front door on our tiptoes, worried that we might wake someone. I crept over to the window of the lounge and peered inside. I felt like a thief, scouting an empty house. There wasn't much to see – a leather armchair, blank walls, a red dot on a plasma screen. Even though I was outside, I could still smell the musty carpet, see the spores of mould on the bathroom tiles, the wormed apples that lay on the ground in the back yard. What was inside now was unimportant to me, the place was still there, and at that moment I felt like I could ring the bell and enter and retake my place at the kitchen table or go into my old room and no one would mind.

A hall light came on. Shit, I said. Let's go, you said. We ran through the long grass, dandelions and weeds and back to the front gate. And there it was. The rock. Not the rock from the beach, another rock, but the same size, the same shape. A grey basalt rock this time, with white veins running through it. It was in exactly the same place, just as I remembered it, holding the iron gate open, like it always did, like it had done since we moved in, battered by rain and wind, blasted by sun, always there, constant, solid, still, like the old man at the garage. No one ever lifted that rock. For a while when I was a kid, my family experimented with leaving the gate closed, without the rock, letting the gate bang against the iron fence three times, but after a while the rock returned. It needed to hold the gate in place. Look, it's Rock, you said, pointing. Yes, I know. Looks the same. It's been there since we moved in. 1984. That's thirty-seven years. Where did you get it? you asked. I've no idea.

And at that moment, I wanted to pick up the rock, feel its grain against my palms, its weight strain my forearms, its roughness chip my fingernails. I realised that I'd never held that rock before and didn't have any rocks or bricks from our old house. Why is it, I asked myself, that we live in places for so long, where our skin and hair shed, and yet we don't take anything of the building with us? The building stays, and we leave. What remains is a shell that used to house us, cocoon us, protect us.

I wanted to take Rock, to remind me of that house. At that moment it meant so much to me, as if keeping it close to me would remind me of my childhood home. My mother would soon be gone to Australia, and I'd probably never come back here, and if I held it to my ear I'd hear the sounds of the house, the classical music, the arguments, the bells from the church opposite. But I didn't. I left it holding the gate open, where it had always been. Maybe it was better that way. You crouched down and flicked your mobile on and shot, the flash filling the night sky like a beacon, blinding me. Rock, you said. Now other Rock has a friend.

He didn't let me take Rock, you said, the moment we walked through the front door when we got back to our home in London. What rock? my wife asked. Ahhh, just some rock they found on a beach. They have plenty of other rocks. Empty your pockets. I don't want to, you said. Come on, show your mother what you brought back, they're beautiful. But I wanted to have Rock, and you wouldn't let me. Why didn't you let them take this rock? my wife asked. There's no way we'd have got it through security. It was massive. You could have let them try, no? No, we were rushing. I had to get the sand out of the car, fill it up, take it back to the car rental place, which is bloody miles from the airport, and we were late. I had no time for the rock. But I don't understand, why didn't you at least try? OK . . .

I said goodnight to you later that evening, you curled up in bed, Kindle lighting your tired eyes, my cardigan and shirts that you like to wear scattered across the floor, school uniform tossed on the back of a chair, your stones on your desk, shining under a lamp, all in a row in size order.

I enjoyed the trip, you said. Glad I came. Don't worry

about Rock. I'd like to go back one day and then we can get another rock. Do you think we'll find that beach again? I'm not sure, I said. It was hard enough to find it the other day, let alone next time, if there is a next time. Let's try, you said. Maybe next summer. We can go swimming. I'll bring towels, I said.

And as I turned off your light and closed the door, I knew that I'd be lying to you if I said that we'd go back to that part of Ireland again, to those beaches, to feel that washed air fill our lungs. I didn't want to spoil the memory of that beautiful day and the stones we found, the ones we took and the ones we left behind. Even if we did go back, we'd argue about where to walk and what time the tide would come in and where we'd have lunch.

I sat on the stairs outside your room and a strain of guilt rose within me, that I'd somehow done you wrong but also done myself wrong by not taking the rock. I didn't tell you that I'd wanted to drive through Dublin alone that evening so I could discard the rock so you wouldn't have to do it, as I knew that you'd get upset, as you don't like throwing things away, but it didn't work out like that and at that moment I missed Rock as much as you did. I knew I couldn't have taken the rock from outside my old house, but the white rock – who really would have cared and why, why did I not let you take it? It was only a rock, but it was your rock, our rock, and I felt that I'd torn something from you, just as my connection to the beach, our old house, the ram's skull was torn from me, and I wouldn't see them again. I had to get it back. I had to have it near me. I had to feel the sharpness of its edges in my palm, the sand under my fingernails. I had to see its brightness in my eyes. I had to lick the salt from its crevices. I had to grip it and smell the dripping ferns. I had to hold it to my ear and hear the sea, the rush of the wind. For you. For me.

Quickly I googled 'petrol station, Swords Road, Dublin', my fingers banging the keyboard like a hammer. There it was: the Maxol garage, a picture of the hoover machine next to the breeze-block wall filling the screen of my laptop. I flicked on my phone and dialled.

Hi, I called earlier about a rock I was looking for? Is the manager back from his break? I asked. One moment, the voice said. It's that same fella calling . . . I heard the voice shout. Hello, a new voice said. Hi. Mister, we've got your rock.

Mayfly Girl

Yvette Naden

There's red in my hair / Naked, slick / I already know 1,000 words / Number 1,001 is 'breath' / It's a word I can taste, and I see it etched above me / My mum wears a rabbit's foot while breastfeeding / Dad sucks a fag in the car park / He comes in at odd intervals, an interlude in a four-act play or an advert on TV / I've never watched a film but the hospital TV is grainy and loud / Sepia tones, like the actors have been dipped in wax / All the women wear shoulder pads and the men say 'spaz' and hit their wives / Dad returns / Smoked-salmon skin bunching beneath his shirt / He asks where my penis is.

I roll out of her arms and onto a bike / Only five minutes spent with stabilisers / Puppy fat dribbles down my legs and onto the pink pedals / John's by the traffic lights / He's in the year above and smells like lemon sherbets / Hair as blue as his Chopper, he waves / I'm catching up, feet brushing the pavement / Mum has stopped pushing me / She's standing on the green, by a sign which says 'No ball games' / Hands clasped in prayer, she's waiting for my dyed hair, my nose rings and make-up / She's waiting to find boyfriends in my bed / She's waiting for my bike to motorise / She's waiting for a lower-back tattoo, perhaps a snake or a skull with a bandana / Maybe I'll get a snake's skull that wears a bandana / The traffic lights are red / John blows me a kiss / He falls and scrapes his knees on the road / He's crying / His mother runs to him / 'Rub some butter on it,' she coos, owlish and small / By the time I've crossed the road, my legs drag along the ground / I'll be taller than my father soon.

The bike gathers rust in the garage / My legs are far too long / I'm a full English breakfast, dripping grease and fat / My hair is lanky but Mum says she won't dye it / 'That stuff ruins your roots,' she says and slips to the salon to erase the grey / It's strange / It happens overnight / My mum becomes Mother / Mother becomes a shrug and an eye roll and a '*She* wants me home before dinner' / And Mother becomes Annie because it makes her twitch, as if her birth name is a curse I've uttered / I call her Annie more than Mother now / In minutes, Dad becomes Father / I'm frowning at his knock-knock jokes and I no longer wonder how many astronauts it takes to change a light bulb / I poke holes in his novelty socks and drop his mugs on the tiled floor / Shout back when he calls me 'young lady' and says I shouldn't stay out so late / The whole speech is there / 'No boy is good enough for my daughter' / You have no idea / He turns away when my lips meet hers, Brittany the Barista / She smells like overripe plums / Her skin is just as squishy / She squeezes me in bed / She pinches me till fat comes out, spitting and white like chicken strips / She goes from

Brittany the Barista to Brittany, my love / My parents won't pay for the wedding.

Father becomes Daniel / Daniel, who listens to Van Morrison and burns the risotto / He waves at Brittany's shadow as we head out / I find my first grey hair during a driving lesson / A woman with jaundiced eyes offers suggestions / When I stall at the roundabout, she sighs / 'The test will be hard,' she says / She's right next to me, but I'm alone, sweating against the leather / Following a sat-nav twelve years out of date / Brittany is too young to drive / I tell her this'll be good for us / I'll take her to Coverack, with its high-domed sky and that hostel with a staircase made from the mast of a Cornish shipwreck / 106 sailors dead / Daniel wants me to start paying rent / Brittany, too, he adds / 'Since she's always here' / Mum leaves early / She comes home late with her tight, tight legs / The outline of her sanitary pad is visible through the spandex / Maybe I should tell Daniel she's fucking her instructor / I wonder when we all became such clichés.

Sun licks the rear fields / They're building again / Affordable housing for the London boys / Tired of the city / The folds of my skin hide sweet wrappers and cynicism / Happens with age, you know / Annie and Daniel, Mum and Dad / They're sat in the garden / Crucified on deckchairs, drinking mocktails / They look like mouthwash from this distance / Tiny cups of acid green and red / 'Cool mint' my arse / My tongue burned for days after that supermarket-brand bottle / The same burn when you inhale dry ice / Brittany takes me to see it / At the Studio Club on Moreton

Street, the drinks cheap and the men cheaper / The music is swollen with bodies and sweat and Brittany's bellowing, getting the words wrong / I go home early.

We lie on the grass beneath the gazebo / Daniel is Dad again / He hired himself out for our one-minute wedding and Mother helped me write my vows / They got the music mixed up and ABBA played / 'A happy accident,' says Brittany / Must be that post-wedding delusion / It'll pass soon / 'Look here,' she says / She passes me her phone / And there's a Facebook post listing everything we couples should be doing / 1) Being comfortable enough to discuss poo / 2) Wearing each other's clothes / 3) Buying a cot / We only manage 5 out of 25 / Brittany's dress is smothered in grass and soil / There're nettles in my hair / I look like Puck from *A Midsummer Night's Dream* / It's more than that / Brittany runs her fingers through me / I shed like a retriever / Those clumps of white and grey.

'I should dye it' / The bench is cold beneath us, a welcome respite from the heat haze / Papier mâché children cry when they mistake ice cream stains for bruises / 'You look good,' says Brittany / Apparently, being in a relationship makes you a liar / Still, we hold hands whilst walking home / The sky stretches thin, canvas-like / Purplish and red, like a wound scabbing over / Mother becomes Mum again as she asks about my day and my wife and the tingling in my bones and finally calls it arthritis / 'Happens to us all,' she says / I laugh / Brittany slaps my arm / Her Bambi eyes / Wide and searching and fearful, hoping this will pass / Hoping I'll be fine.

You can imagine it, can't you? / Waking up, mistaking her toothbrush for yours / Moaning at petrol prices and silently judging the dead-eyed kid behind the counter as he inspects your card / 'You'll have to enter your PIN' / Become a yo-yo for your boss: promotion, demotion, large office, airing cupboard / Answering to a twelve-year-old in a three-piece suit / I sit and swallow.

And on the plane, they offer all kinds of hypothetical food / 'I'll have the chicken,' I say and roll my eyes at the 'Sorry, we're out' / Brittany beside me, and she stays that way until the beach / She rubs lotion into my back but I still end up sunburnt / I push her in the water / The sandbanks are draped with seaweed / We take some home.

And we're taking pictures of the *Mona Lisa* / Neither of us understands her smile / What we do get is a warning from a rectangular security guard who smells of sandalwood and baby shampoo / Brittany nearly steps into the railing because she's checking the map / I grip her arm like it's an axis and pull myself up.

Grandma visits in the dark / We're back from Paris, with its honeycomb flats / Back from New York, where Brittany and I played kiss chase in Central Park till a woman shook her head / Not in front of her kids, she said / I wonder what Gran will think when I tell her.

Gran / With a saddle-bag face, all leathery and hard / She has the family nose, which curls towards her cleft chin / She perches on the bed / Downstairs, Brittany is ironing /

My parents supervise.

There are wine gums in her pocket / Hairy, like tiny orange- and lime-flavoured rats / She holds one out / I've lost my appetite.

She visits when I'm writing my own name on the walls, just to keep it there / 'It's like living in an old folk's home,' she says when I ask her who she is and why she's here / A reminder / She's Grandma.

It makes me wonder how I'm supposed to react / If I'm supposed to smile because my bladder is loose and my bones crack.

Brittany is a furnace against me / Everything exists in extremes / Too hot, too cold, too much, too little / Enough / Brittany's hands are coals, bursting and burning / Her knuckles swell to cradle me.

She holds my hand / Asks if I've recorded the Grand National / She's placed a bet, you see.

She sits up / Rubs her face while I count the pockmarks on the ceiling / Some are shaped like moons.

The bed is cold / I wriggle, hunting for leftover warmth.

What a day.

Communion

Avril Caprani

On the eve of my thirtieth birthday, my mother phoned to tell me she was joining a commune in Wexford. I'd been meaning to disconnect the landline for months.

We were half-dressed when I picked up. I looked at Mike, his face a freshly shaven pink, his smile verging on anxious as he tapped his slender wrist, mouthing 're-ser-va-tion'. I said hello and Mam said she wouldn't keep me, she'd only wanted to wish me a happy birthday. She wouldn't get the chance to call tomorrow – there was the move to consider.

The restaurant in Soho was a sparsely lit room of five or six tables, where none of the food came on a plate. Mike couldn't understand why I was so upset.

'You barely ever see your mum,' he said, spooning up his deconstructed seaweed appetiser with gusto. 'This might be really good for her.'

I reminded him that he'd never met my mother. This was a woman fiercely dedicated to her own company, a dutiful cultivator of silences. Her description of her recent lifestyle choices had been terse. Something about a community farming initiative she'd found online, the sunshine, the sea air, and no, before I asked, she hadn't given them any money. She'd write to me once she was settled. An image of her floated to the forefront of my mind: the self-righteous, cardiganed stand of her, in amongst a flock of dreadlocked strangers, the whole lot of them screaming together into a field of cows.

Arrangements were made one cobwebbed, hungover morning some six months later, with Mike steadfastly ignoring me as he completed his daily stretch routine. I flew from Gatwick early, the gates of the airport thick with queues. Mam had written only once since she'd run away, telling me nothing more than what she'd been up to that one particular day in April. She wasn't overly fond of lentils yet. Now, it was summer, and Ireland resurfaced in the distance again – uncommonly green and hopeful when viewed from above. I pressed my face to the Ryanair window.

The sun had half-set into a murky orange jelly by the time I reached Wexford's coastline. To my surprise, the location of the commune wasn't the ramshackle cluster of cottages I'd envisioned. There were no hammocks. The sea was nearby, but out of sight from the entrance to the tall, upright, ivy-covered building I found instead – not unlike the parochial house from the village back home. I parked the rental car alongside the others in the neat driveway.

A teenager in a faux-fur bucket hat opened the door to me. She was pudgy and beautiful, her eyes like two black stars.

'I came to see my mother,' I said. 'I think she lives here.'

'You aren't staying, are you?' She stared pointedly at my bags.

A thin drizzle licked the back of my neck. 'I don't know, to be honest.'

'Jesus. Come in, then.'

She left me in the hallway, her gold platform runners squeaking against the dark wood as she sloped away. I stood waiting at the foot of a long staircase, eyeing myself in the gilt-framed mirror on the wall opposite. Back in the old house, there had been a small, square mirror hung in the light-choked hallway. Mam disapproved of its use, or any other form of what she used to call preening. She appeared at the top of the stairs now, a look of pure alarm on her lovely face.

'Sinéad?'

'Hi, Mam,' I said. 'Sorry, I should have warned you.'

I hugged her, returning her three stiff pats on the back before letting go. Her head was shorn, the buzz cut a soft, dandelion-tuft silver. For the first time in my life, she had a tan. Mam took in my own dark head, my temples peppered with coarse grey hairs. Examining the fine lines around my eyes, she appeared relieved. 'You've completely grown up,' she said.

She told me to leave my things in the hallway, rolling her eyes as I extracted my handbag. We came to a large, yellow kitchen at the back of the house, warm and smelling of onions. The teenage girl was there, scrolling on her phone at a banquet-style table almost the width of the room, her schoolbooks spread out in front of her. Two scruffy-faced men were sat at the other end, their voices raised in frantic conversation. Our entrance went unacknowledged.

'I'll make tea,' Mam said, turning towards the many labelled jars along the countertop and squinting. 'We'll have the nettle.'

We sat in two squat armchairs in the corner, and I stared into the bitter, unstrained leaves.

'What are you doing here, Mam? This isn't very you.'

'And I suppose you have a good idea of who I am now, do you?' she said.

'You're a teabag person, for a start,' I said. 'Do you not miss home at all?'

'No,' she said. 'I don't. The house was unmanageable, and I didn't see a soul from one week to the next. I came here for a rest.'

I glanced towards the table, where both men now stood bickering. Tinny dance music was bleating from the girl's phone. 'And is it restful?'

'I didn't expect you to understand, Sinéad, and I definitely didn't expect you to come here. So please, just leave it be.' Her mouth had set into a familiar, resolute line. 'Let's find you a bed for tonight. We'll ask Gerry.'

Gerry was ensconced in a tiny room upstairs, a makeshift office lined with books. He was the narrowest man I'd ever met, his ginger-grey hair all raked to one side. His nose was lengthy as well, and crooked, so that his glasses sat lopsided on his face. While the men in the kitchen were dressed in a vaguely hippieish manner, with ill-fitting linen shirts and saggy trousers, Gerry looked even more like a retired schoolteacher than my mother did.

'We don't usually allow guests during the first year,' he said, addressing Mam.

'That seems strict for a commune,' I said.

'We're not a bloody commune.' He rubbed his eyes. 'We're a community-led project. We're trying to build a sustainable life here, together.'

'And how does that differ from a commune, exactly?'

'This isn't necessarily a spiritual endeavour,' he said, 'despite what the younger lot think. There are no leaders here.'

I took this second point for bullshit – there was always a leader. Gerry and Mam went back and forth about the rules for a while, folding and unfolding their arms. He was unprepared for my mother's will, had obviously never come up against it. He took a navy-blue logbook from the shelf behind him and wrote down my name.

Mine was a four-bed dorm room. Mam had been given her own space, Gerry explained, since she had proven her commitment to the three Rs – Respect, Ritual and Renewal. I raised an eyebrow in my mother's direction while she stared obstinately at the beds wedged against the wall. I knew better than to ask her to share.

They left me then, discussing something they called 'the early gathering'. I shoved my bags under the only free bed, a single with hospital corners under the window. The night air blew in over my head, soft and close, and two missed calls from Mike blinked up at me from my phone. I considered the various reactions he might have to the news that I was sharing a different bedroom, before dialling my father's number.

'Well, did you find your mother before she found herself?' he said.

'I don't know why I bothered coming,' I said. 'Mam's grand. Maybe I'll drive out to you tomorrow instead?'

133

'Ah, give it a few days. If you feel you're going a bit mad then, we can work something out. Make sure she doesn't have a voodoo doll under the bed, all right? I'm starting to feel tingles.' He chuckled loudly to himself, still blissfully unaware of my mother's sheer lack of concern for him. I hung up and got under the clean, white covers, turning to face the wall.

By the end of that first week, I had little understanding of how the project worked, nor did I know what any of them did all day. Over in London, I'd left my entry-level finance job in the lurch, with the sufficiently formless excuse of a family emergency back home. My new roommate Elise, a gap-toothed marine biologist from Zurich, informed me that she spent most of her time scouting out places to be alone with her boyfriend Billy, who was new to the men's dorms. 'Did you not come here looking for the opposite of privacy?' I asked her.

'I think I came for the sex,' she said, picking the raisins from her muesli.

We shared our room with Mimi – the youngest member of the community at fifteen years old – and her mother, Pearl. Pearl was a genuine earth-mother type, all silky floor-length dresses and Stevie Nicks hair. She was unofficially in charge of the kitchen, organising most of the huge group meals, as well as monthly moon-worship sessions. Gerry from the office appeared to both fancy and despise Pearl. I was glad to share a room with her, since she proved an undecided point for me.

My mother worked hard in the vegetable garden, where we were each required to spend at least five hours every day. Wexford ants marched zigzaggedly along the hot, cracked pavement behind the house. I drank grainy coffee on the homemade decking, watching Mam crouch among the lettuces.

'You were never into this sort of thing before,' I called out.

'I never had the patience before,' she said, emerging from the greens to approach me. Her fingernails were dirty.

'Who bought our house?' I asked.

'Hughie O'Leary bought it for his daughter's family,' she said. 'He wanted to have them close by. That man is more than a touch selfish, I can tell you.' She slid past me into the shade of the kitchen.

Elise's boyfriend Billy wore a biker jacket and scuffed Doc Martens to work in the garden. Across the back of his raw, sunburnt head, the word 'cherish' was tattooed in bold, looping letters. Billy had one conversational response, applicable to any given situation:

'Those carrots are coming up nicely, Billy.'

'More power to ya, girl!'

'Honestly, Billy, I don't get it. She's acting like she barely knows me. I came here hoping I could make things better.'

'And more power to ya.'

One Sunday after my garden care, I found Mimi in our bedroom, her hair newly dyed a violent purple colour. I knew her mam was at the nudist beach down the road. I'd been invited along twice over breakfast.

'Do you ever drive anywhere?' Mimi asked, after several minutes of ignoring me. 'You know you're still allowed to go places, yeah?'

'I know that,' I said, enlightened. 'Do you want to go somewhere?'

She looked up from her phone, gorgeous and glum. 'McDonald's?'

We drove for almost an hour. She ordered a Big Mac meal and two ice creams, one for me. We sat in the car, avoiding the teenagers hanging around the tables inside.

'Do people in school ever say anything to you, about where you live?' I asked.

'You live there too,' she said. 'They don't say much. Some people think it's cool, but most of them just don't talk to me. One of the girls used to call my mam a slut.'

'Did you tell your mam that?'

'Nope. She'd just tell me to write it on a piece of paper and burn it or some shite.' She grinned at me. 'Do you have any kids?'

I studied my sticky, McFlurried hands. 'No, not yet.'

'Good,' she said. 'Don't do it. It's not a good thing to do.'

I thought of Mike's carefully timed conversations, the photos of his brother's beautiful, pristine children on our fridge in London. It had begun a few months ago, this new desire of Mike's, like something he'd read a *Guardian* article about and wouldn't let go. We couldn't get near the park without a row. I'd never managed to tell him why it was I came over to England in the first place, over ten years ago now. He'd never taken it upon himself to ask.

Mimi broke the silence with a loud, contented burp. We made our way home, the rental car smooth and soundless on the warm asphalt.

*

My one real friend was Aidan, a short, sturdy fella who dressed exclusively in old GAA jerseys, blue jeans, and flipflops. He was from Kildare, and I found him rolling cigarettes out on the decking one evening, his tongue deftly tracing the paper. We got to smoking together in the coolness of night, once he'd come sauntering downstairs with his tobacco pouch, an apple and a knife.

'What did you make of the dahl?' he asked, coaxing a glow from the tip of his rollie.

'My bowels move with reckless abandon these days,' I said.

He passed me the cigarette and began paring the apple into thin, juicy slivers. They landed on a plate between us. 'Should be used to it by now.'

'Do you not miss the odd night out?' I asked him, the smoke tearing at the back of my throat. 'Pints in a beer garden on a night like this?'

'I can't say I do. Not at this stage,' he said. 'I was a drinker when I got here. I'd start the night in the beer garden, but then I'd wake the next morning after piddling some stranger's bed. It got to be too much for me.'

'Surely some drinking goes on here as well,' I said. I heard Mike's distant tutting, his disdain for my thirst and my newfound, wonky accent.

'There's less of it than you'd think, you know.' Aidan pitched the apple core into the near-dark sky. 'The place started off as a kind of sober house, according to Gerry. But it was tucked too far into the arse of the country to be of much use to anyone looking to make a go of it in the real world. So, then all sorts started turning up eventually.'

I thought of my mother, diligently working away at a

one-thousand-piece jigsaw with Elise and Billy at the table inside.

'Your mam's a lovely lady,' Aidan said, watching me. 'I hope she finds some peace here.'

I snorted, turning away from him. Below us, the night-dew on the grass was fragrant and clean. He put a hand on the small of my back. 'You can stay too, you know,' he told me. 'You don't have to go anywhere unless you want to.'

Sex made it a little easier to understand the appeal of the place. It was a loose, youthful sort of sex that I felt was from another lifetime – all nerves and stronger limbs. The need to be furtive made the act of it more basic – no time for showboating – with Aidan's quick, appreciative kisses on my stomach as he worked to pull down my jeans. I came loudly in the garden and the bathroom and his bedroom upstairs. He worked wonders with his hands.

I couldn't tell if Mam had noticed. Her eyebrows arched involuntarily whenever she saw me, an old tic from my schooldays. On dinner duties together in Pearl's kitchen, she'd place her hands on my waist to move past me, and I'd feel fifteen years old and useless again. I watched her peel Maris Pipers with a tremor in her hands, and a lump lodged like a spud in my throat. I asked Pearl not to put us cooking together again, citing familial tension, and she reluctantly complied. 'Us mammies don't always get it right, Sinéad,' she told me, slicing carrots into perfect half-moons. 'It doesn't mean she doesn't love you, petal.'

I took Mimi to McDonald's most weekends, where we sat in the car with the windows open, baking in the smell of burger grease and petrol. Outside, summer was drawing hesitantly to a close, the magpies in the car park promising all sorts of joy and sorrow ahead.

Sometimes I'd buy a couple of naggins of whiskey on the way home, dribbling the dregs into my teacup later on. I wondered if Aidan could smell it off me; if he'd challenge me to change my ways. He didn't pass any comment. Mam continued to speak to me at mealtimes in a perfunctory sort of way, or just after her shift in the garden, when her cheeks were ruddy-red and her eyes bright like a child's.

One night, I dreamt she was out weeding in our old back garden. She knelt in the shadow of the house, her eyes lowered, with blood streaming from her hands into the soil. I woke sweating, Pearl snoring opposite me, and made my way to Mam's room across the landing, my T-shirt damp and clinging to my back. There was no answer to my small knock on the door. Inside, the room was warm and musty, the heavy curtains drawn. When my eyes adjusted to the dark, it was Aidan I recognised first, the sturdy shape of him fitted snug around my mother. They were both breathing deeply, almost in unison. Mam was turned to face him, the soft down of her head cradled into his chest.

The next evening, I stood in the doorway of her room again. Mam sat perched on the edge of the bed.

'Dad called yesterday,' I said.

'And how was he?'

'He was wondering what the hell I'm still doing here. I promised I'd visit himself and Yvonne ages ago.'

'Well, that might be a nice idea. I've enjoyed seeing you, I'm sure your father would as well.'

'Do you want me gone now, Mam?'

'I never said that, Sinéad. But I have been wondering

about that boyfriend of yours in London. Are you not missing him?'

'What about your old life? You've been here a lot longer than I have.'

'I didn't have much of one,' she said. The conversation was left untethered for a moment, flapping like the sheets out on the line. 'Look, I know you came here to save me, and I appreciate it, even if you were a bit late. But this is it for me now, really. I'm grand where I am.'

I looked down at her lovely face, drooping with gravity. I wanted her to know that I still required saving. I needed Máire Ní Bheoláin, the headteacher I'd ignored in school, fiercely stalking down corridors in awful court shoes. Silent at home, only ever speaking to me in the creaking softness of a language that made me feel so guilty, I'd beg her in the end to please, please stop.

I looked at this new, placid mother of mine who could have been anyone's.

'More power to ya, Mam.'

Outside, the car unlocked with a firm, familiar click in the balmy darkness. The tray of seedlings Gerry had asked me to pick up in town sat cloaked on the back seat. Faint chatter came drifting up from the house, while somewhere close by, the sea lapped mournfully at the blue-black shore. I waited again, for someone to stop me from doing something I might regret, before the engine hummed and I was moving along capillary country roads. On the N11, a hare lay bleeding, exposed on the hard shoulder, and I wished for someone to tell.

Turf Smoke

Rosaleen Lynch

I stink of turf smoke, adolescence and manure and though
Ladies' Day at the horse races is a good day for a girl to go
stealing, with the women smelling of kindness and the men
only aware of bits of women that don't include handbags
on arms, I watch the races instead, feel every stride of the
horse I've picked to bet the money I've not got on, as if I'm
on the horse's back willing him forward, he can do it, I
know he can and he does, but I've lost my chance, while
everyone's stood still, looking through binoculars, and now
they all move, and the ladies, corseted stomachs in,
shoulders back, heads high, can't see anything past their
waists as they walk, but I avoid them on grass when they
look down, worried about their shoes, and try to catch them
in the milling, when their long skirts brush against one
another, in the gathering around the turf accountant,
collecting their winnings or placing their next bet, and if
this doesn't work I stand, hand out, pulling my small stature
smaller, as if the hunger I feel is eating me away before
their very eyes, and my posture allows them room to think
about how they might share their good fortune to raise up

and save someone who could have been them, but guilt can do strange things and have a lady turn away as fast as it can have them fill my hand with coins, and my story is always the truth, that yes, my wild copper hair has a natural curl, and yes my mam and da know I'm here and no I can't do anything else for food between harvests, and I don't turn and ask what they do for food, because at least I don't have to wear a corset, I'm only bound by family values and beliefs, which moor us only long enough to Ireland to learn we must go and take them with us when we leave our Irish shores, when stories of turf roofs, monks and peace persuade Mam that going will be best for us, and I think one land must be much the same as the next if there's one letter difference in islands, between the Iceland we leave for and the Ireland we leave behind, not that any of us has a choice, we all follow Da, whether we like it or not, it's only in lifeboats women and children go first, but before we go, to pay for passage, we save the turf one last time, and that last night in Ireland, you can tell we've been down the bog cutting turf, not by the red cheeks or the state of us, but by the smell of us, even keeping upwind of the peat fire, smoke finds us, waters our eyes, seasons our food and soaks into our hair and clothes like the incense from Sunday Mass, and the turf even gives me my name, Mona, which Da says is the old English for moon, and Mam says is the old Irish for turf, and I was born under the moon by a turf fire, weighing little more than one of the sods I'd wrap in a shawl and call 'baba' when I was too small to help at harvest, when my brothers would try to scare me with stories of the convict, who instead of going to prison was sentenced to work in the bog, and Mam would shush us, as she kept the fire going, the tea in the kettle hot, soup warm in the pot, spuds baking in embers and us warm in the evening, taking the youngest always, to wrap in her skirts to sleep, and I was torn between wanting to grow up to be like her or like Da and I thought back then that I had a choice, and I thought I'd grow up and nothing would change, and everything would be the same cycle, like when we'd be worn out by work begun as fun, and every year forget the back-breakingness of it all by next harvest, and want to do it all again, when every Easter wasn't just the end of Lent, when we finished fasting and tried to understand the priest's prayers about resurrection and the symbolism of potatoes, it was the countdown of the longer days to summer harvest time, whether it was in the bog or the potato fields, we all came together with the clouds in the sky for our roof and the soft earth for our floor, our church needing no walls or windows and no one had to kneel on hard stone flags or put money in the collection plate to help the priest build a bigger church while people went hungry or left Ireland for better lives, while convicts got shipped to Australia or were made to work the bog, and I thought about this when we came home from the bog that last night, after Da had his bath and the three of us climbed in after, to play with the turf dust that floated in soap scum with blades of grass and a broken daisy chain, with Mam's complaints singing out about the three damp piles of clothes stepped out of on the floor, that she picks up to take out back to shake the bog from them and sniff and noticing nothing offensive, hangs them up in the night air and later on the rack over the range, putting vests and knickers in the bath after us and taking three clean sets from the airing cupboard for us to wear to bed, our hair drying faster than we want by the range and me offering to go out and bring in a bucket of turf to keep the fire going as it is, but Da says the fire needs to sleep too and sends us to our prayers and to top and tail it in a bed for three, and I don't know how it's going to change, but stay the same, how in the future I'd not share a bed or bath with my brothers or strip off in front of them, or wear the same clothes, that our work as children, footing the turf into sod steeples, would as adults not only change but be divided, me, tending the bog fire, my brothers digging with slanes and cutting the turf of another land, across the sea in Iceland, and turf smoke would be all that connected us in this new land of ice and fire, transporting us and in us, in our food, lungs, hair and clothes and our stories, on the dog-sled trailer ride home, bouncing over ruts, thrown together like dried turf sods in a fire, and our coming together in the fields to be wedged apart again at the same Sunday Mass, when we're once more scrubbed clean, sitting still and upright, in rows of church pews on different sides of the aisle divide, the boys in caps and me in a shawl covering my hair and wearing the only dress that I have, a cast-off of Mam's, draughty in winter, even with the underskirt tied together between my legs, with the only comfort being that the priest might feel it worse, standing up there in his draughty cassock at the altar, his back to us, chanting the Lord's prayer in Latin while we all say it in Irish even in this foreign land, and in the fields I pick the potatoes by hand, though I want to use a fork to stab the unbroken ground, climb up on it to push deeper, hang on the handle to lever the earth to reveal the potato treasures bursting into light, but it was no job for a girl I was told and when I said I wanted to cut the turf, in this new land with new ideas, my brothers said I was mad, that they'd trade places with me if they could, but they still took up the slane and left me raking the ashes, thinking about how even convicts got to work in the bog, and so I built, lit and tended the fire and though Mam told me that without fire there'd be no food, no turf cut and in turn no fire, food or turf, I knew we could all go up in smoke, could be cutting the ground from under us, yes, Pope Pius talks of a combustible earth, says the priest one Sunday, when the talk of turf wars begins and other wars too and at night I'm colder by the bog fire than those further away getting warm from their work, and when cold numbs or locks I get up and circle the fire to get my blood flowing, but still I'm chilled and I see it's time for the dogs to be fed, so I take the bucket and each of the dogs gets their portion and I drive the sled to the peat water trough so they can have their fill, and as no one's looking, I drive them on, through the bog that's not being dug, and I let them have their head, willing them forward, they can do it, I know they can and they do, and now I've my chance, and we turn at the boundary's fence and I gauge the distance back to be the length of the annual sprint in the dog-sled races and I time myself in Irish seconds, *a haon, a dó, a trí, a ceathair* . . . and I do it in just seven seconds over the record but maybe I've miscalculated the distance, and I tie up the dogs again and return to the fire, warm now, and drop back to the ground, tuck my skirt under me, wrap my shawl about me tighter and try to keep warm from my work, and I pick up a stick, from the same tree the men's slanes had been fashioned, but a twig in comparison, thinner, lighter and appears weaker but does a woman's work, and bends and springs back when other more rigid ones might snap, my female slane, and with it I mix tea leaves from the caddy into the hot water of the hanging kettle, stir the soup pot, prod spuds, turn them in embers to stop rawness one side, charring the other, all infused with the peat, even the tea, and I am most of all but I remember that on Sundays the priest doesn't smell of bog, but of priest, and in Iceland he wears his ceremonial clothes more often than our Irish holy days and he carries a wooden staff, like a shepherd's crook he says, but he doesn't smell like a shepherd, and at harvest time he comes to bless the work at the bog in a freshly ironed and starched collar and cassock, and I count thirty-three buttons down the front and notice he's replaced his skull cap with a square tea-cosy kind of hat that smells of mothballs if you get close enough, and he rests his foot on a slane, where it's been placed for him by Da, and he blesses it and pushes down into the turf until only the wooden handle sticks out like a cross in a grave and everyone claps but me, because he's the first person in a dress I've seen cutting the peat and I watch as he speaks to the other men about fighting for your beliefs like the men in the far-off trenches and he reaches into one of his hidden pockets and takes out a bright-white handkerchief, maybe for his nose or to wipe his brow of the heat but he wipes his hands, as if the very touch of the common man's slane is too much for one of his standing and I turn my back on him that day and don't don my dress and shawl again on a Sunday to sit and listen to him from any of the pews, I am not his lamb and I would not grow up to be a sheep, instead I'd go the convict way and become a wolf, or the nearest I could get to one in Iceland, the red sheepdog, or '*madra rua*' I call what I think is a fox that we start breeding for sledding to have our 'horse' races where I don't have to steal into the audience, where I'm taking part in the race, and though Da says it's just because I'm light enough for speed, Mam says he could easily put my younger brother on but Da told her I was the best musher he'd seen on snow and land and bog and I know it's because, just like the dogs and the horse, I want to run, I will myself forward, I can do it, I know I can and I do, I take every chance, whatever they say, while my brothers become men at the wrong time, and one by one they race off to war swapping the bog for a foreign fighting land and their slanes for guns and it doesn't matter that the island we left and the island we left for are neutral, they still give up peace for war, two brothers join the British army together and one fights the civil war in Spain and not one of them comes back, and when I'm out flying through the countryside with the dogs, I imagine they've survived and are living long and happy lives and if they don't, it was up to them, they had all the chances and each chose to put down the slane and pick up a gun, and the priest calls them martyrs, but I say just because God gave up his only son doesn't mean everyone else has to do the same, sure the priest has no children so he can't feel the pain like Mam, unless maybe if he was nailed to a cross, a suggestion I make to him, in the line waiting for bones at the butcher's when he says how proud I must be of my martyr brothers, and I offer to carry out the crucifixion myself if he'd help by climbing up onto the cross and holding his feet and hands in place long enough for me to climb the ladder on each side, and though it would be hard for me, a woman, to do it on my own, I could with his help, and then my anger's polluted when my brothers come back to me in the smoke, reminding me of our Irish bog summers saving the turf, with its dried-dirt earthy smell we carry with us, long after we grow out of our childhood clothes and swap bare feet for adult shoes, and long after the turf and my brothers are gone, and the priest is safely in the ground, and when the last breath of bog fire is spent, diluted in our blood, like the rivers of red iron of the Icelandic bog, to travel into the afterlife on, to reclaim the land with our lives, when the stick and slane and staff can lie down together, equal in the earth we're buried in, making turf together, all sides of the divide, and in the future to be dug up once more, like stories to light the fires of new generations, and the metal, from our guns and crucifixion nails, will lie and rust, as useless to the earth as they ever were, and no one will fight over a sod of turf again and I tell Da this as I take his dying body on one last sled ride with the dogs and he tells me of his fears of not preparing me for the journey of going from Miss to Missus and of his pride that I'd found a different way, as Musher, and I know when he starts to talk of turf that there's not long now, and I push the dogs to go faster, willing them forward, we can do it, I know we can, there's still a chance, and I drive them on, that we might try to outrun the turf smoke one more time.

Contributors' Bios

Shazia J. Altaf is a writer from Middlesbrough, in North East England, from a working-class background. She won the 2021 Creative Future Writers' Award Platinum Prize for her short story 'Essential Thread', which was published in CFWA's 2021 anthology, *Essential*, and which she performed at the Southbank Centre, London. Her debut novel, *Jammed Ascent*, which she is currently editing, was shortlisted for the inaugural Primadonna Prize in 2021, and her work was also listed for the 2021 Exeter Short Story Prize. Shazia has been awarded an Arts Council England National Lottery Project Grant.

Avril Caprani is a writer from Co. Meath, Ireland. Her work has previously appeared in *An Capall Dorcha* and *Sonder*. She currently lives in London.

Kate Ellis is a writer and ex-bookseller based in London. Her short fiction has been published in the *Open Pen Anthology*, *The Mechanics' Institute Review* and *The London Short Story Prize Anthology* among others. In 2020, she was longlisted for the Deborah Rogers Foundation Award for her debut novel. She runs the Brick Lane Bookshop Short

Story Prize and hosts the BLB Podcast. Twitter: @katesmalleyelli.

Imogen Fox is a fiction writer from Manchester. She has an MA in creative and life writing from Goldsmiths, University of London, where her short story 'The Swimming Pool' won the 2022 Pat Kavanagh Prize. She is now working on developing that story into a full-length novel.

Emily Gaywood-James grew up in the Midlands and spent time living and working in France, Spain, Denmark and the USA before settling in London in 2016. Her writing has been published in anthologies and literary journals including *City of Stories Home* and *Tipping the Scales*. She is currently working on her first novel.

Giovanna Iozzi is completing a creative writing PhD at Goldsmiths, University of London, and is a winner of Goldsmiths' Pat Kavanagh Prize. Her stories have been published in *Ambit*, the *New Writer*, the Brighton Prize *Rattle Tales* collection, *The Gold Room* anthology and by Exeter Writers. Her first novel explores maternal disintegration, and she is working on a memoir. Website: joiozzi.com. Twitter: bristlingnarratives@gioiozzi.

Dr **Denise Jones**, HonDLitt, FRSA, Freeman of the City of London, studied graphic design, was a primary school teacher and has worked with the bookshop that she co-founded since 1978. She lives in Cable Street and was an elected Labour councillor in Tower Hamlets from 1994 to 2022. Denise strongly supports the arts and is a board member of Rich Mix, Young V&A, Trinity Buoy Wharf

Trust and Mulberry Schools Trust. She is Deputy Chair of the Portal Trust, where she chairs the Grants committee, and Chair of the Aldgate & Allhallows Foundation. She has served on the boards of the Arts Council, Museum of London, Whitechapel Art Gallery, Create London, Lee Valley Regional Park Authority and other trusts.

Bonnie Lander Johnson is Fellow in English at Newnham College, Cambridge. She has written academic books about Shakespeare and Renaissance culture and is now writing fiction and creative-critical prose. One of her stories was shortlisted for the 2021 V. S. Pritchett Prize and her creative non-fiction has appeared in *Hinterland* and *HOWL*. She is working on a biography of Shakespeare, a fenland farming novel and a collection of stories about mixed-race love.

Miki Lentin started writing when travelling the world with his family a few years ago. He completed an MA in creative writing at Birkbeck, University of London, in 2020 and has had a few successes along the way, notably as a finalist in the Irish Writers Centre 2020 Novel Fair and achieving second place in Fish Publishing's Short Memoir Prize 2020. He has also been published in *Litro*, *MIROnline*, *STORGY* and others. He longs to open his own café again in the future.

Max Lury recently graduated from the creative writing MA at UEA, where he was the co-recipient of the 2022 Curtis Brown Award. His fiction has been previously published in *Lighthouse Journal*, and is forthcoming from Tar Press. He is currently working on his first novel, *No Ghosts*.

Rosaleen Lynch is an Irish community worker and writer in the East End of London with words in *CRAFT*, *SmokeLong*, *Jellyfish Review*, *Ellipsis Zine* and *Mslexia*, shortlisted by Bath and Bridport, winner of the HISSAC and Oxford Flash Fiction Prizes and can be found on Twitter @quotes_52 and 52Quotes.blogspot.com.

Yvette Naden was born in France but now resides in the UK where she attends the University of York. Her work has featured in the *Wizards in Space* anthology, *The Roadrunner Review* and the *Hive South Yorkshire* magazine. When she isn't writing, she can be found trying to resuscitate her houseplants.

Hannah Retallick is from Anglesey, North Wales. She was home educated and then studied with the Open University, graduating with a first-class BA (Honours) Arts and Humanities (Creative Writing and Music) degree, before passing her creative writing MA with distinction. Her work has been shortlisted/placed in several international competitions. https://www.hannahretallick.co.uk/about

Martha Sprackland is an editor, writer and translator from Merseyside. She runs Offord Road Books and is poetry editor for CHEERIO Publishing. A collection of her poems, *Citadel* (LUP, 2020), was shortlisted for the Forward Prize for Best First Collection, the Costa Poetry Award and the John Pollard Foundation International Poetry Prize.

Judges' Bios

Anne Meadows is an editorial director at Picador Books. She loves the intensity of the acquisitions process, the rigour of an edit and the buzz of watching a book she's laboured over find critics, readers, prizes and (hopefully) posterity. While in her previous role at Granta Books, Anne worked with Gwendoline Riley, Margo Jefferson, Hiromi Kawakami, Sayaka Murata, Mariana Enríquez and Sandra Newman.

Huma Qureshi is an award-winning writer. Her memoir, *How We Met: A Memoir of Love and Other Misadventures*, was published in January 2021, chosen as one of *Stylist*'s best non-fiction picks for 2021, while her debut short-story collection, *Things We Do Not Tell the People We Love*, was published in November 2021, chosen as the *Guardian*'s Book of the Day. She was shortlisted for the Brick Lane Bookshop Short Story Prize 2020, for her story 'Small Differences', and won the *Harper's Bazaar* short-story prize in the same year. She is now writing a novel, which will be published by Sceptre in 2023.

Chris Wellbelove joined Aitken Alexander as an agent

in 2017 and was made a director of the agency in 2018. He was shortlisted for Literary Agent of the Year at the 2019 British Book Awards. He represents Daisy Johnson, Vanessa Onwuemezi, Kayo Chingonyi, The Secret Barrister and many others.

Judges' Quotes

On the Anthology

'The BLB SSP longlist is testament to the breadth and imagination of a new generation of writers, and the elasticity of the short-story form. We read stories that were funny, sexy, deeply sad, and very strange. We read them not knowing a thing about their authors, finding ourselves amazed again and again by the talent on display. It's a wonderful list.'

Anne Meadows

'Exceptional stories, each so startlingly different, yet all stay with you. A true celebration of the short-story form.'

Huma Qureshi

'The stories on this longlist showcase the range and excitement of the form – read them for their invention and imagination, and for their abilities to move, surprise and amuse.'

Chris Wellbelove

1st Prize

Missy Starling – Imogen Fox

'*Misery* through the perils of social media and an obsession with a pop star. It's genuinely tense and the narrator has a strong, memorable voice. It's a little sickening; no one comes out clean.'

Anne Meadows

'I fell in love with *Missy Starling* from the very first line. Such a clever, slick, witty, engrossing story that was so much fun to read. I loved its energy, its slightly sinister edge, the fact that it made me laugh. The pacing and structure were spot on and I loved every part. Outrageous in a good way, this was hands down my favourite story and a truly deserved winner.'

Huma Qureshi

'Refreshingly original. This story has an energy and a sense of humour that grabs you from the first line.'

Chris Wellbelove

2nd Prize

Tipping – Giovanna Iozzi

'The main character's apocalyptic panic is painfully rendered, and her relationship with her long-suffering partner is well done. This is the first thing I've read, published or otherwise, that really depicts menopause.'

Anne Meadows

'A satisfying, urgent and important story, about motherhood, womanhood and climate change, with stand-out imagery that will stay with you.'

Huma Qureshi

'This is clever – making climate change bodily is something I don't think I've seen before, and it's well done. Interesting and thought-provoking.'

Chris Wellbelove

3rd Prize

In Translation – Emily Gaywood-James

'A brief, sweet story of unrequited love. The gaps in language between the narrator and her love interest are well handled. The author also gives us an interesting approach to the narrator's gender and sexuality, both of which are revealed through the misapprehension of others.'

Anne Meadows

'I loved this simple, tender story of unrequited love that felt like it had such heart to it. Wistful and poetic.'

Huma Qureshi

'The writer feels in control of the story – the whole is pretty confident.'

Chris Wellbelove

Shortlisted Stories

Idolatry – Bonnie Lander Johnson

'This is an accomplished, beautifully written short story, with a clear narrative arc and memorable characters. There's real energy to the writing, and the author melds their own work with the Bible passages skilfully. The language is lush and carefully chosen.'

Anne Meadows

'An elegant story; gorgeous writing, with beautiful prose.'

Huma Qureshi

'A clever and moving story. I enjoyed the intertextual elements.'

Chris Wellbelove

Riding Lessons – Max Lury

'A bourgeois dinner party shades into nightmare. This is a funny, twisted story with two genuinely disturbed men at its centre. I felt very sorry for the poor horse, but it also made me think about how much we can really know anyone else, and it's an excellent depiction of the morass of early adulthood; very grisly.'

Anne Meadows

'I lost myself in the writing of this; super-smart dialogue and an astute observation of post-university friendships. A strange story (in a good way) that draws you in with an astonishing, slightly sinister edge.'

Huma Qureshi

'Good writing, and the way the group dynamic is done is brilliant.'

Chris Wellbelove

Whitebait – Martha Sprackland

'A well-written story with a strong sense of place. The two women and the power struggle between them was really interesting.'

Anne Meadows

'Poetic prose, elegant and haunting, with the constant threat of something unsettling. Deeply moving.'

Huma Qureshi

'Good imagery.'

Chris Wellbelove

Longlisted Stories

Clara By Every Name – Hannah Retallick

'There's an interesting gender ambiguity in this story, and a sense of drama and tension. It reminded me of an early Almodóvar film, or the work of JT LeRoy. The language is well done, with a clever use of words ("she weaved her way out of trouble"), while still retaining a voice that feels true to the character and their haphazard life.'

Anne Meadows

'An intriguing exploration of identity.'

Huma Qureshi

'Good on identity/gender/naming, and I thought the characters being on the run was clever.'

Chris Wellbelove

Communion – Avril Caprani

'A really powerful depiction of an unusual mother-daughter relationship. There's a good voice to it, the dialogue is well done; and I was impressed by how the author renders the narrator's sense of melancholy and dispossession. The characters, including the lesser characters, are all really well drawn.'

Anne Meadows

'Remarkably insightful writing about a dysfunctional mother-daughter relationship with an unexpected twist.'

Huma Qureshi

'Nice writing, and I think the setting and dynamics of the commune are well done.'

Chris Wellbelove

Mayfly Girl – Yvette Naden

'So much of a life contained in six pages; dizzying, strange, timelines folding in on one another. An impressive piece of work.'

Anne Meadows

'Poetic, intense, breathless.'

Huma Qureshi

'Admirable ambition.'

Chris Wellbelove

Selling Oil – Shazia J. Altaf

'A powerful depiction of racism and sexism in British culture. The main character is really well drawn, and there's a strong sense of claustrophobia; you're really rooting for her, and the end is crushing.'

Anne Meadows

'Dark and disturbing glimpse of prejudice, questioning belonging.'

Huma Qureshi

'I like the structure here, and the ambition.'

Chris Wellbelove

The Rock – Miki Lentin

'This was well structured, with a clever rendering of time going forward and backwards. I liked the depiction of the teenager, particularly. And the story as a whole has a melancholy sweetness to it.'

Anne Meadows

'A tender exploration of a father-child relationship, and the meaning of home. Moving in its simplicity.'

Huma Qureshi

'Nice writing.'

Chris Wellbelove

Turf Smoke – Rosaleen Lynch

'A coming-of-age story contained in one sentence. There's a strong narrative voice, an ambitious setting, and the history is woven in well.'

Anne Meadows

'Brave, experimental writing.'

Huma Qureshi

'I really like the energy in the writing, and the opening is great.'

Chris Wellbelove

Previous Shortlistees' Quotes

'Winning the competition was such a confidence boost. Validation from other writers, editors and agents pushes you to consider your work as valuable and worth the time that you're putting into it. It was such a joy and an honour and I was so grateful to have won it.'

Aoife Inman, 2021 winner

'I think, quite simply, that the BLB Prize made me feel I might not be entirely insane to try and do this writing thing.'

JP Pangilinan-O'Brien, 2021 shortlist

'I was so excited to be shortlisted for the Brick Lane Bookshop Prize 2021 among excellent writers. It's a really great prize that offers all longlisted authors the opportunity to be printed in the Prize anthology and that is an amazing moment in itself – getting to see your words in print.'

Leeor Ohayon, 201 shortlist

'Entering the Brick Lane Bookshop Short Story Prize was the best thing I did in 2021. I spent so long convincing myself that I wasn't a "real writer" and it is hard to express in words how much being shortlisted in 2021 buoyed my confidence. Seeing my name in print was exhilarating and I got to meet some other lovely and talented writers in the process. I cannot recommend it enough. If you are even slightly considering it, apply! Only good things can come of it.'

Nayela Wickramasuriya, 2021 shortlist

'Writing can feel quite lonesome, strange, insane – so for me, this competition meant: there's something worthwhile about it. Keep at it, said the announcement. Keep at it, said the book on my shelf. And keep at it, said every response from everyone who read my words. Thanks to the Brick Lane Bookshop Short Story Prize, I keep on keeping at it.'

Kieran Toms, 2020 2nd Prize

'Being awarded 3rd Prize in the 2020 Brick Lane Bookshop Short Story Prize by such a wonderful panel of judges was thrilling and special for me. This prize may be relatively new, but it's already establishing itself as a favourite with short-story writers and readers alike.'

K. Lockwood Jefford, 2020 3rd Prize

'Being shortlisted gave me confidence in myself and it also led to much bigger things that were out of my control. It was really important.'

Huma Qureshi, 2020 shortlist

'I'll never forget the launch party: my story, with my name, in so many books in so many hands. All because I walked past a poster in the window of Brick Lane Bookshop and thought, "What's the worst that could happen?"'

James Mitchell, 2019 winner

'An amazing, affirming experience. It was a completely joyous surprise to have my work read and held carefully by the competition team and the judges. It's such a beautiful feeling to know that people have read your work and somehow connected with it, seen something in it and want to celebrate it.'

Isha Karki, 2019 shortlist

Thanks

Every writer who submitted a story to the competition.

The fifty long-longlisted writers who made our job so enjoyable and difficult.

The twelve longlisted writers whose excellent stories make up this anthology.

First readers: Danae Bravi, Andrew Carson, Glenn Collins, Kalina Dimitrova, Chris Ellis, Andrew Everitt, Harry Gallon, Olivia Griffiths, Elinor Johns, Bret Johnson, Jarred McGinnis, Kira McPherson, Tom Norton, Sophia Pearson, Sean Preston, Tamara Pollock, Ayşe Irmak Şen and Adelaide Turnbull.

Second readers: Xanthi Barker and Max Sydney Smith.

Judges: Anne Meadows, Huma Qureshi and Chris Wellbelove.

Denise Jones for her foreword.

Sue Tyley, our brilliant copy-editor and proofreader.

Peter J. Coles, BLB Podcast editor, producer and co-host, plus all of our guests.

Our stockists.

Everyone who bought and read the 2019, 2020 and 2021 anthologies.

Friends and supporters on- and offline, including previous years' longlistees, Open Pen, Spread the Word, Comma Press, Republic of Consciousness Prize, MIROnline, Scratch Books, *Sunday Times* Audible, and many others.

Online listings: writers-online.co.uk, nawe.co.uk, mironline. org, duotrope.com, neonbooks.org.uk, aerogrammestudio. com, christopherfielden.com, pocketmags.com, shortstoryaward.co.uk and nothingintherulebook.com.

Goodreads reviewers.

Clays printers.

Turnaround book distribution.

Brick Lane Bookshop customers for choosing to shop with us and supporting an independent.

Brick Lane Bookshop booksellers Denise Jones, Polly Jones, Kalina Dimitrova, Andrew Everitt, Glenn Collins, Bret Johnson and Ríbh Brownlee, for their support.

www.bricklanebookshop.org

BLB Podcast

The BLB Podcast celebrates and interrogates the short-story form. For each episode, we invite a writer to read from and discuss their work. We ask about their writing and editing processes, getting published and what they're reading.

Hosted, produced and edited by Kate Ellis and Peter J. Coles.

Find us at bricklanebookshop.org, or search 'Brick Lane Bookshop' on Spotify, Apple Podcasts or Pocket Casts.

Guests so far:

Isha Karki   Vanessa Onwuemezi
Aoife Inman   Keith Ridgway
Jarred McGinnis   Irenosen Okojie
Jem Calder
Wendy Erskine
Leon Craig
Niamh Mulvey
Huma Qureshi
Ben Pester